AN ACCIDENTAL
FAMILY

AN ACCIDENTAL FAMILY

BY
AMI WEAVER

First published in Great Britain 2013
by Mills & Boon, an imprint of Harlequin (UK) Limited.
Large Print edition 2013
Harlequin (UK) Limited, Eton House,
18-24 Paradise Road, Richmond, Surrey TW9 1SR

© Ami Weaver 2013

ISBN: 978 0 263 23683 5

Harlequin (UK) policy is to use papers that are natural, renewable and recyclable products and made from wood grown in sustainable forests. The logging and manufacturing process conform to the legal environmental regulations of the country of origin.

Printed and bound in Great Britain
by CPI Antony Rowe, Chippenham, Wiltshire

For the Wicked Muses:
Chelle, Jodie, Marcy and Rae.

Thank you for all your help. I love you all.

And for Dale, who believed. xo

CHAPTER ONE

THE STICK WAS pink.

Lainey Keeler squeezed her eyes shut, lifted the test with one trembling hand, then peeked with her right eye only.

Yup. Definitely a pink line. Maybe she needed to check the instructions to be sure....

Oh, God. How had this happened?

Okay, so she knew the technicalities of the how. In fact, she knew the when. Lord help her, that was the kicker.

Her eyes swam and her stomach rolled as she reached for the test box anyway, knowing what she'd see there. Knowing the result would read the same as the four other sticks—all different brands—in the garbage.

Knowing she'd been screwed in more ways than one.

So this was the price she paid for one night of lust infused with a heavy dose of stupidity.

She slumped on the cold tile of the bathroom floor and let her head thunk on the vanity door. Hysterical laughter bubbled in her throat and she pressed her fingertips to her temples. Did it count, fifteen years after graduation, that she'd finally bedded the star quarterback? The same one she'd nurtured a killer crush on all through high school?

And managed to conceive his baby?

"And here I thought I had the flu," she said to her calico cat, who observed her from the doorway. Panda's squinty blink in response could have meant anything. "Why didn't being pregnant occur to me?"

Single and pregnant. Right when she was starting a new business and her life couldn't be more unstable.

What would her parents say? She winced at the thought. At thirty-three, she was supposed to be burning up the career ladder. Instead, much to her family's chagrin, she burned *through* careers.

Chewing her lower lip, she took a last look at the pink line, then tossed the test stick in the trash with the others. Five pregnancy tests couldn't be wrong, no matter how much she wished it. She needed a plan.

"A plan is good," she said to the cat in the doorway. Panda meowed in response. Shoot, what was she going to do? She stepped over the cat and hurried into the small hallway, facing straight into her pocket-sized bedroom. Panic kicked up a two-step in her belly. She'd need a bigger place. The cozy one-bedroom apartment above her shop, The Lily Pad, worked beautifully for one person and an overweight cat. But adding a baby to the mix…? Babies needed so much *stuff.* She laid her hand on her still-flat belly. *A baby.*

Good God, she was going to be a mother.

She clenched her eyes shut and willed the tears away. What kind of mother would she be? Her ex and her family told her over and over she tended to be flighty and irresponsible. A baby meant responsibility, stability.

What if it turned out they were right? She certainly hadn't demonstrated good judgment on the night of her reunion.

The thought sliced her to the core and she took a deep breath. No time to cry. Not when she had a shop to open in a few minutes. Beth Gatica, her friend and employee, was already downstairs. She swiped at her eyes, tried to think.

"Where do I start?" she wondered aloud, trying to get her head clear enough to think.

A doctor. She'd need a doctor. Her usual doctor happened to be a friend of her family's, so she'd definitely have to head over to Traverse City. Since she felt better with something to do, she reached for the phone book.

"Lainey?" Beth's voice came through the door connecting the apartment to the shop. "Are you okay?"

Lainey fumbled the phone book and caught sight of herself in the small mirror next to the door. Dark blond hair already escaping from her ponytail? Check. Dark circles under her eyes? Check. Pasty skin? *Yikes.* Wasn't there supposed to be some kind of pregnancy glow? "I'm fine," she called. "Be right there."

"Okay, good. Because we've got a problem."

Well, of course they did. Lainey marched over and yanked open the door, almost grateful for the distraction. "What kind of problem?"

"Come see." Beth turned and hurried down the stairs, long dark curls bouncing. The fresh, cool scent of flowers hit Lainey as they entered the workroom. Beth tipped her head toward the older of the two walk-in coolers. "It's not cold enough, Laine. It's set where it's supposed to be, but it's nearly twelve degrees warmer in there."

"Oh, no." *No.* She needed the cooler to last another year—like she needed the van with its iffy transmission to last another six months. Preferably twelve. A headache began to pulse at the edges of her brain at the thought of her nearly empty bank account. Using only one cooler would mean reducing inventory, which meant possibly not being able to meet the needs of her customers. Which meant less income. And she couldn't afford to lose a single cent at this point.

To say The Lily Pad operated on a shoestring budget was to put it optimistically.

She pulled open the door, even though she didn't doubt Beth. She could feel the difference as soon as she walked in. She tapped the thermostat with her finger. Maybe it was stuck somewhere? She should be so lucky.

"Call Gary at General Repair," she said to Beth. "See if he can get us in today."

"On it." Beth hurried to the phone.

Lainey headed to the working cooler to do some rearranging. Some of the more delicate flowers would have to be moved over.

She tamped down the spurt of fear and worry that threatened to explode. No point inviting trouble, and Lainey figured she had enough to fill her personal quota. She closed her eyes and inhaled the fresh, green scent of the flowers, with their overtones of sweet and tangy and spicy. It always, always relaxed her just to breathe in the flowers.

But not enough, today, to rid her of her worries. About choking coolers. About babies. Lainey smothered a sigh. If she'd stayed home two months ago part of her predicament wouldn't be here. She'd invited trouble. Or, more accurately, trouble had invited her.

Of course she hadn't turned him down.

"Gary will be here at eleven," Beth said from behind her. "Want me to help move things?"

Lainey glanced at her watch. An hour and a half. "Sure. We'll just move a few for now. Let's group them by the door so we can open it a minimum of times." The colder it stayed in there, the better for her bottom line. She couldn't afford to lose a cooler full of flowers.

"Are you okay, Laine? You're awfully pale," Beth commented as she lifted a bucket of carnations out of the way.

Lainey sucked in a breath. Should she tell Beth? They'd been friends for years. Beth wouldn't ridicule her for her mistake with Jon. It would feel so good to tell someone....

"Lainey?" Beth's head was cocked, her brown gaze worried. "What's going on?"

"I'm pregnant," she blurted, and burst into tears. Beth hurried over to her, nearly knocking a bucket over in the process.

"Honey, are you sure?"

Lainey nodded and swiped at the tears. "Pretty sure." Five separate pink lines couldn't be wrong. Could they? "I'll have to go to a doctor to confirm it, though."

"Oh, Laine." Beth hugged her, stepped back. "How far along? I didn't know you were seeing someone."

Lainey closed her eyes. *Here we go.* "Well, I'm actually not. I'm about eight weeks along." She'd let Beth do the math.

"So that's—oh." Beth drew out the word and her eyes rounded. "Your class reunion."

"Yeah." Lainey couldn't meet her friend's gaze. Her poor baby. How could she ever explain the circumstances of his or her conception?

"So who's the daddy?"

"Jon Meier." Lainey could barely say his name. "We…ah…hit it off pretty well."

Beth gave a wry chuckle and opened the cooler door, a load of calla lilies in her hands. "So it seems."

"I have to tell him, Beth, but he lives so far away. Plus the whole thing was pretty forgettable, if you know what I mean. We used protection, but obviously…" She shrugged and swiped at her leaking eyes again. "It didn't work." An understatement if she'd ever heard one.

"He's not father material?"

"I don't know." It wasn't as if they'd discussed things like personal lives. "Plus he lives in LA. He's in some kind of entertainment industry work. He's not going to pull up and move back to Northern Michigan." He'd made his contempt for the area crystal-clear.

"Sometimes having a kid changes that," Beth pointed out.

"True." Lainey didn't want to think about it. "But I think we were pretty much in agreement on how awkward the whole thing was." So much for sex with no strings attached. The baby in her belly was a pretty long string. The length of a lifetime, in fact.

She wanted to bang her head on the wall. What had she been thinking, leaving with Jon that night? Was her self-esteem so damaged by her divorce she had to jump on the first guy who smiled at her?

Best not to answer that.

"I think you'll be a wonderful mom," Beth said, and Lainey's throat tightened.

"Really?" She couldn't keep the wobble out of her voice. Beth's confidence touched her. Her family would look at her being single, pregnant and nearly broke and lose their collective minds. She shoved the thought aside.

"Of course. You're wonderful with my kids. Now, let's get this finished before Gary gets here."

* * *

"It could go at any time?" Lainey could not believe she'd heard the repairman correctly. A year—she only needed twelve measly months. Why, oh, why was that too much to ask? "Are you sure?"

"Yes. We can cobble this along for a few more months. But you are definitely going to need a new unit." Gary's lined face wasn't without sympathy.

She took a deep breath. "Do what you have to, Gary. I need it to last as long as possible."

The repairman nodded and returned to the cooling unit.

Beth stood at the counter, ringing up a large bouquet of brightly colored carnations. A great sale, but not nearly enough to buy a new cooler. Or even a used one.

"Thank you. Have a great day," Beth said to the customer as he exited the shop. To Lainey she said, "What's the news?"

"We're going to need a new cooler. Sooner rather than later, probably." Exhaustion washed over her and she sank down on the stool behind the counter. "Even used, that's not something I can swing yet." Or possibly ever. No cooler, no business. No business, no cooler.

No business, no way to provide for the baby.

A wave of nausea rolled through her at the thought. Another failure. This one could be huge.

"Oh, man." Beth leaned on the counter. "Well, let's see. We've got the Higgins wedding coming up. We need more weddings. The funeral business has been picking up. That's good. Maybe...."

She hesitated, and Lainey knew what her friend hadn't said.

"Maybe if my mother sent business my way we wouldn't be in this predicament," she finished. "I know. I agree. I've asked." The answer, while not in so many words, was that the florist her mother used had been around a lot longer and wasn't in danger of folding. The implication? Lainey would fail—again.

Beth winced. "I know you have. I just wish she'd support you. I'm sorry I brought it up."

"It's okay. It's the truth. I don't know what will change her mind." Lainey stood up. "Let's finish getting the deliveries ready."

As Lainey gathered flowers and greenery she wondered if she'd let her business go under rather than ask her parents for a loan. They'd give her one, with plenty of strings attached, and she'd have to crawl to get it. This was supposed to be her chance to prove she could make something of her life without advanced degrees or a rich husband.

Right about now it didn't seem to be working.

Gary came out of the cooler, toolbox in one hand, invoice in the other. "You're all fixed up, Ms. Keeler. Can't say how long it'll last. Could be one month. Could be six. I'm sorry I don't have better news."

"The fact it's running right now is wonderful," Lainey said. "Thank you. I appreciate you coming on such short notice."

"Anytime. Have a good day, ladies." He left the store and the bell above the door chimed, its cheerful sound mocking Lainey's mood. She looked at the amount on the invoice and sighed.

She'd known when she bought the shop nine months ago there were no guarantees on equipment. Even in her current financial bind she didn't regret taking the plunge. This shop felt right to her in a way none of her other jobs ever had. Right enough, in fact, that she hoped to someday buy the building outright.

Working steadily throughout the morning, they completed their orders. The repair seemed to be holding for now, thank goodness. Lainey slid the last of the arrangements into the back of the van and closed the door. "All set, Beth. Hopefully we'll get more this afternoon."

"Fingers crossed." Beth climbed in and turned the ignition. She leaned back out the window. "I'll stop at Dottie's Deli and grab lunch on the way back. I think we've each earned a cheese-cake muffin after this morning."

"Mmm." Lainey perked up at the thought. Everyone knew the calories in Dottie's heavenly muffins didn't count. "Sounds wonderful. Thanks."

She held her breath as Beth thunked the old van into gear and drove off. Relief washed over her. After this morning she'd half expected the thing to go belly-up out of spite.

"Don't borrow trouble," she reminded herself as she turned and went inside.

The chime of the door caught her attention and she hurried to greet the customer.

Fifteen minutes later she started on a new arrangement, this one for a new mom and baby at the hospital. They really needed more of this kind of business—more happy occasions like...

Babies.

Pregnant.

Lainey gulped and gripped the edge of the worktable, her eyes on the array of delicate pastel flowers she'd gathered. She only had about seven months to stabilize her shop and get ready to be a new mom herself. A *single* new mom.

Seven months.

No one could ever accuse her of doing things the easy way.

Ben Lawless pulled into the driveway of his grandmother's old farmhouse and stared. Same white paint, black shutters. The wide porch was missing its swing, but two rockers sat in its place. The two huge maples in the front yard had dropped most of their leaves. Funny, he'd been gone for so many years but this old house still felt like home.

He frowned at the strange car parked behind his grandmother's trusty Buick. Last thing he wanted was to talk to anyone other than his grandma, to deal with friendliness and well-meaning questions. Acting normal was exhausting.

He pushed open the truck door, stepped out and scanned the layout of the front yard. Plenty of room for a ramp, though some of the porch railing would have to be removed, and it would block one of the flowerbeds lining the house's foundation. He kicked at the leaves littering the cracked walkway. The uneven concrete posed a hazard even to an able-bodied person. Why couldn't Grandma admit she needed help?

Why did you assume she didn't need it?

His self-recrimination didn't get any farther as the front door opened and framed his beaming grandmother in her wheelchair. He tried not to wince at the sight. She'd always been so tough, strong and able, and now she looked so small. He moved up the walk and the stairs to the porch.

"Grandma." He bent down to give her an awkward hug in the chair, afraid to hold on too tight. "How are you?"

She hugged him back firmly and patted his face. "I'm good. Making the best of this, I hope." She studied his face for a moment, her clear blue eyes seeing too much. "I'm so glad you're here. Not sleeping well?"

He straightened, not surprised by the observation. "Good enough."

She gave him a look, but dropped the subject and rolled back into the house. "Where are my manners? Come in, come in. I want you to meet a very good friend of mine."

Ben braced himself as he followed her across the familiar living room to the kitchen. Hopefully this friend wasn't one of the mainstays of Holden's Crossing's gossip mill. Last thing he needed was word getting out and people asking him questions or making accusations. He stopped dead when he looked into the cool blue gaze of the gorgeous—and young—blond at the kitchen table.

"Ben Lawless, meet Lainey Keeler. Lainey, this is my grandson. The one who's a firefighter in Grand Rapids." The pride in Rose's voice made Ben's stomach twist. "Lainey was a few years behind you in school, Ben."

No way. *This* was his grandmother's friend? Long dark blond ponytail, a few strands loose around a heart-shaped face. Clear blue eyes, smooth creamy skin. Full breasts a snug pink tee didn't hide. He gave her a brief nod, forced the proper words out. "Nice to meet you."

Her smile curved, but didn't reach her eyes. "Same here. Rose has told me so much about you."

"Did she?" He tensed at her comment, then forced himself to relax. It didn't mean she actually knew anything. He rested his hand on his grandmother's thin shoulder. "Grandma, I'm going to bring in my things, okay?"

Lainey rose. "I'll walk you out." She leaned down to plant a kiss on his grandma's cheek and gave her a hug. "I'll see you in a couple of days, Rose."

"Don't work too hard, honey," Grandma said, and Ben nearly laughed. If he remembered correctly, none of the Keelers had to work. They'd been given anything and everything on the proverbial platter.

Ben caught a whiff of her scent, something floral, as she moved past him. Since he'd gotten boxed in, he followed her out into the cool early October night.

Once on the porch, she turned to him with a frown. "She's glad you're here."

"And you're not."

Those big blue eyes narrowed. "I'm not sure. She's been struggling for months now. Where were you then?"

Temper flared at the accusation in her tone. He'd felt bad enough once he'd realized how much help his grandma needed. He didn't need this chick sticking her nose in, too. No matter how hot she was. "She isn't big on admitting she needs help." Seemed to run in the family.

Lainey gave him a look that said he was full of it and stomped off the porch. "She's in her eighties. How could you not come visit and check on her?"

Guilt lanced through him. "She always said she was fine, okay? I'm here now." Why did he care if this woman thought he was a total heel?

She shrugged. "You still should have checked on her. How far is it up here? She's so proud of you. But you never bothered to visit."

Even in the dim light he saw the sparks in her blue gaze, the anger on his grandmother's behalf. "I'm here now," he said, his own temper rising.

"Till you leave. Then where will she be?" She spun around and strode across the yard.

God help him, he couldn't pull his gaze off her tight little tush. She climbed in the little car and slammed the door. The spray of gravel that followed her out to the road said it all.

Well, great. He'd managed to tick off his grandmother's hot little friend.

Ben shook his head and stepped off the porch, walked to his truck to get his bags. He'd done something far worse than that. His best friend was dead, thanks to him, and any problems with Lainey Keeler were not even on his list of important things. It made no difference what she thought of him.

Back inside, his grandma frowned at him. "Why were you rude to Lainey?"

But of course it would matter to Grandma. He scrubbed a hand over his face. "I'm sorry. It's been a long day. I didn't know you two were friends."

"We are. We met awhile back when she volunteered for Senior Services and just clicked, as you young people say. She comes out every Wednesday. More if she can. I didn't think you knew her." His grandmother's eyes were sharp on his face.

"I don't. Just knew *of* her. She was four years behind me in school, as you said. How are you feeling?"

She studied him for a second, then seemed to accept the change of topic. "Every day is a little harder. I'm so glad you're here and can make this old house a little easier to live in. I don't want to leave it."

These last words were spoken in a soft tone. Ben knew this was the only home she'd lived in with his grandfather, her husband of fifty years. Her best friend.

The kind of love and relationship he'd ended for Jason and Callie.

Pain pounded at his temples and he closed his eyes. He shoved it down, locked it back into the deepest part of him he could. Thing was, that place was nearly full these days.

"You won't have to leave, Grandma. You'll have to tell me what you'd like done besides the ramp. Even in the dark I noticed the walk out front has seen better days."

Her smile was rueful. "A lot around here has seen better days, Ben."

"We'll get it fixed up, Grandma. You won't have to leave," he repeated.

"I know. I'm very grateful to you." She maneuvered the chair toward the living room. "Let me show you to your room. Well, partway anyway."

Ben started to say he knew where it was, but of course she'd have taken over the downstairs bedroom after the arthritis in her hip got too bad. "Which one?" There were three upstairs.

She stopped at the base of the stairs and looked up, the sorrow and longing clear on her face. "The back bedroom. It has the best view and is the biggest room. Lainey freshened it up for you. Dusted, clean sheets, the whole shebang. The bathroom is ready, too."

His grandparents' old room.

"Okay. Tell her thanks for me."

Grandma backed her chair up and gave him a little smile. "You can tell her yourself. Didn't I mention she visits a lot?"

He stared at her. *Uh-oh.* "Grandma. I'm not interested."

She slid him a look and her smile widened. "No one said you were."

He'd walked right into that one.

Smoke filled the room, smothering him, searing his lungs, his eyes, his skin. God, he couldn't see through the gray haze. A cough wracked him, tearing at his parched throat. He couldn't yell for his friend. Where was Jason? He couldn't reach him. Had to get him out before the house came down around them. A roar, a crack, and a fury of orange lit the room. The ceiling caved in a crash fueled by the roar of flames. He spun around, but the door was blocked by a flaming heap of debris. Under it, a boot. Jason. Coming to save him.

Ben woke with a start, his eyes watering and the breath heaving out of his lungs as if he'd been sprinting for his life. Where the hell was he? Moonlight slanted through the window, silver on the floor. The curtain stirred in the faint breeze. He sat up and pushed himself through the fog of sleep. Grandma Rose's house. Had he cried out? God, what if she'd heard him? Shame flowed over him like a lava river. He stepped out of bed, mindful of the creaky floor, and walked down the hall to the bathroom near the landing.

No sound came from downstairs.

He exhaled a shaky breath and went into the bathroom. He'd been afraid of this—of the nightmare coming. He had no power over it—over what it was, what it did to him. No control.

He turned on the squeaky faucet with unsteady hands and splashed cold water on his face. There'd be no more sleep for him tonight.

CHAPTER TWO

LAINEY WALKED INTO Frank's Grocery after closing the shop and pulled out her mental shopping
list. Nothing fancy. Just sauce, pasta, shrimp,
some good cheese. If she had more energy she'd
make the sauce from scratch, but not tonight. So
far the hardest thing about being pregnant was
being so tired at the end of the day. She grabbed
a basket from the stack and headed for the first
aisle.

She came to a dead stop when she spotted the
tall, dark-haired man frowning at the pasta sauce
display.

Oh, no. Ben Lawless.

She didn't want to chat with Rose's grumpy
grandson. He'd made it pretty clear he wasn't interested in being friendly. Since he stood smack
in front of the sauce she needed, though, she'd
have to talk to him.

He glanced up as she approached. For a heartbeat she found herself caught by those amazing light green eyes, by the grief she saw searing through them.

What the heck? She cleared her throat. "How are you?"

He tipped his head in her direction, his expression now neutral. "Fine, thanks."

His uninterest couldn't have been clearer, though his tone was perfectly polite.

"I just need to get in here." She pointed to the shelves in front of him. He stepped back, hindered by a woman and cart behind him, and Lainey slipped in, bumping him in the process. A little shiver of heat ran through her. "Sorry," she muttered, and grabbed the jar with fingers that threatened to turn to butter.

She managed to wiggle back out, brushing him again, thanks to the oblivious woman behind him who kept him penned between them. She plopped the sauce into her basket and offered what she hoped passed for a smile. "Um, thanks."

"No problem," he murmured.

She turned around and hurried out of the aisle, unsettled by both the physical contact and his apparent loss. So Ben had a few secrets. That flash of grief, deep and wrenching, hit her again.

Rose had never mentioned anything. Then again, why would she? She'd respect her grandson's privacy. It was one of the things Lainey loved about her friend.

It only took a few more minutes to gather the rest of the ingredients. Her path didn't cross Ben's again, and she unloaded her few purchases at the checkout with relief.

Outside, she took a big breath of the cool night air, and some of the tension knotted inside her eased. Fall was her favorite time of year. A mom and small daughter examined a display of pumpkins outside Frank's and her thoughts shifted back to her baby. Next year she'd be carving a pumpkin for her five-month-old. Oh, sure, he or she would be too small to appreciate it, but despite the precariousness of her position the idea gave her a little thrill.

She deposited the bags in the trunk and slipped into the driver's seat to start the car.

Click. Then nothing.

Oh, no. Maybe if she tried it again....

Click.

She leaned forward, rested her head on the steering wheel, and fought the urge to scream. Not owning any jumper cables, she'd have to go back into Frank's and find someone who did. While she was at it she'd hope like crazy the problem was simply a dead battery, and not something expensive. She yanked the keys out of the ignition, grabbed her purse and got out of the car. One thing was for sure—she'd push the stupid car home before she'd ask her parents for help.

She nearly collided with Ben coming out of the store.

"Whoa," he said, checking his cart before he ran her down.

Before she could think, she blurted, "Can you help me?" Her face heated as he stared at her. "Ah, never mind. I'll find..." She gestured vaguely behind him but he shook his head.

"What do you need?"

"My car won't start. I think the battery's dead. The dome light's been staying on longer than it should and it didn't go off at all this time. I don't have any jumper cables." Realizing she was babbling, she clamped her mouth shut.

He nodded. "Where are you parked?"

She pointed. "There. The silver one." Which he no doubt already knew, since he'd seen her in it the other night. "The space in front of me is open."

"Okay. Give me a minute. I'll pull around."

He walked off and she stared after him. *Shoot.* Why hadn't she found someone else? On the other hand, the whole process wouldn't take very long. Then she could be on her way back home to fix her dinner and curl up in her bed.

The wind picked up, skittering dry leaves across the parking lot, and she tucked her hands under her arms to keep warm as she went back to her car. She propped the hood open as a big black truck rumbled into the empty spot.

Ben got out, cables already in hand, and went to work on her battery. Even though she knew how to hook them up—her mother would be appalled—she let him do it, because it was easier than having his carefully bland gaze on her.

He glanced up. "Do you know how to do this?"

Something in his tone made her bristle. She lifted her chin just a bit. "Actually, I do. I can even change a tire."

His mouth twitched in what could have been a prequel to a smile. "Good for you."

Before she could reply, a voice shrilled nearby. "Lainey? Lainey Keeler, is that you?"

Ben returned to the battery and the fragile moment was shattered. Lainey internally groaned as she turned to see Martha Turner, one of her mother's best friends, hurrying toward her.

"Hi, Mrs. Turner."

"Goodness, what are you doing?" The woman peeked around Lainey and frowned. "Do your parents know you have car trouble? I just left your mother at the Club. Have you called her yet? I'll never understand why you traded in that cute little coupe your husband bought you for—for this." She fluttered her hands at the car.

Not offended, Lainey bit back a laugh. She had to be the only person who'd ever traded in a new car for a used one. "Of course I didn't bother either of them, Mrs. Turner. It's really not a big deal. Just a dead battery."

Behind her, Ben cleared his throat. "Sorry to interrupt, but I need to start the truck now. It's loud."

"Okay." She gave Mrs. Turner an apologetic smile. "It was nice to see you."

Mrs. Turner's gaze went to Ben, reaching into the cab of the truck, then back to Lainey. "You too, dear. Take care."

Lainey could almost see the wheels turning in the other woman's head and imagined her mother would get a phone call before Mrs. Turner even made it inside Frank's. She sighed. She'd get her own call in a matter of minutes after that, and spend a half an hour calming her mother all over nothing.

So much for a relaxing evening.

Ben came back around and stood, hands in pockets, staring at her engine. Finally he lifted his gaze. "What did you trade in?"

Not exactly sure how to interpret his tone, she spoke carefully. "A Mercedes. After my divorce."

She didn't mention the sleek little car had been a bribe—an attempt to keep her in the marriage. Getting rid of it had been a victory of sorts. One of the very few she'd managed.

She caught a glimmer of amusement in his eyes. "That's funny?"

He rocked back on his heels. "Not the divorce.

The car. I wouldn't think—" He stopped and she frowned.

"Think what?"

He looked at her, amusement gone, and seemed actually to see straight into her. The full effect of his gaze caused a funny little hitch in her breath. "I think you can start the engine now," he said, and she swallowed a surge of disappointment.

Which was crazy. She didn't care what he thought of her.

She slid into the car and tried not to notice when he braced one arm on the roof of the car and the other on the top of the door. When he leaned down she got a tantalizing glimpse of the smooth, hard muscles of his chest through the gap in his partially unbuttoned shirt.

Her mouth went dry.

"Go ahead and see if it'll start."

His voice slid over her skin and she gave a little shiver. She caught a whiff of his scent— a yummy combination of soap and spice. A little curl of heat slipped through her belly. She reached for the ignition and hoped he didn't notice her shaking hand. The engine turned over on the first try.

"You should be all set now," he said, straightening up. "Drive it around a bit to let the battery charge up."

"I will. Thank you," she said, and meant it. "I appreciate it."

He shrugged and stepped back. "No problem. I'd have done it for anyone."

Her little hormonal buzz evaporated. Of course he would. After all, she'd practically attacked him when he came out of the store.

"Well, see you around," she said, and he gave her a nod and then disappeared around the front of her car.

She sat for a moment, waiting for him to unhook the cables, and gave herself a reality check. She was two months pregnant. Being attracted to a man right now couldn't be more foolish—and she'd learned the hard way what a poor judge of men she was. She'd paid dearly for that mistake. Her focus was her shop, her baby, and making her life work without her parents hovering over her, waiting for her to fail.

Clearly these pregnancy hormones threw her off balance.

The hood of the car dropped with a thud and

the sudden glare of headlights made her blink. With a little wave, in case he could see, she put her car in gear and backed out of her spot, then drove the long way through town back to her apartment. Ben stayed a respectable distance behind, but the thoughtful gesture gave her an unwelcome frisson of warmth.

Under his gruff exterior, Ben Lawless was a gentleman.

Somehow that made him more dangerous.

Lainey let herself in to her apartment, not allowing herself to glance after Ben's truck as he drove on by. Her phone rang. She dug it out of her bag and checked the display. Ah, here was the call she'd been dreading.

"Hi, Mother," she said into the phone, as a purring Panda wound between her feet.

"Hi, dear," Jacqui Keeler trilled. "I'm almost there. Let me in, love."

That hadn't taken long. Mrs. Turner must have really run up the alarm if she was getting a visit, too. Lainey dumped her bags on the counter with a little more force than necessary. "Here? Why?"

"Can't I simply visit with my daughter?"

Oh, if only. "Of course, Mother. I'll be down in a sec."

She dropped the phone back in her purse and glanced around her cozy space. Her apartment was neat, for all the good it did. It would never meet her mother's standards, no matter what. She'd learned that years ago.

She hurried down the front stairs to unlock the street-level door just as her mother walked up.

"Lainey." Jacqui kissed her cheek, her usual cloud of sweet perfume tickling Lainey's nose. "You look tired."

She bit back a laugh. If her mother only knew. "Thanks," she said dryly as the trim older woman swept past her up the stairs. Jacqui, as always, was impeccably groomed. She wore a pale pink suit and her smooth blond hair swung smartly at her chin. Lainey ran her hand down her ponytail and tried not to feel inferior in her non-branded jeans and tee shirt.

Damn it. She'd given that life up. But, oh, sometimes she did miss designer clothes.

"Have a meeting tonight, Mother?"

"I did." Jacqui tucked her monster-sized bag securely under her arm, as if she expected to be robbed right there on the stairs. "For the Auxiliary at the hospital. The gala."

No surprise there. For all their differences, Lainey still admired her mother's energy. "When is it?"

"Two weeks. Don't forget you are expected to be there."

Right. Just what she wanted. "Who did the floral arrangements?"

"Gail, of course. She does a lovely job."

Implying that The Lily Pad didn't. Disappointment clogged her vision for a moment. Lainey opened her mouth, snapped it closed. Frustration rushed through her. She'd never get through to her mother until the woman took her seriously. When would that be? What would it take?

"You really should move back home, honey," Jacqui said, her gaze drifting around the living room. "We have plenty of space. You could have your old room back. We'd love to have you."

Lainey stifled a sigh. More like they'd love to micro-manage her life into one that met their standards. Been there, tried that, failed spectacularly.

"I know you would. I'm very happy here,

though." Lainey saw her mother's hand twitch, as it did when she was stressed. "Can I get you something to drink?"

"No, thank you." Jacqui perched on the edge of the sofa, the monster bag set primly on her lap, and Lainey sank down on a nearby chair. "Now, I received a disturbing phone call from Martha this evening. You had car trouble? Why didn't you call?"

Lainey smoothed her hand on her jeans. "It was nothing. Really. A dead battery. Not worth bothering you over. Rose's grandson Ben helped me out."

Jacqui's tone turned chilly. "Yes, Martha said you were with a man."

Lainey nearly choked. "Standing in a parking lot while someone was kind enough to jump my battery is hardly being with a man." Though she'd certainly had visions of another kind of jumping, but those were best kept to herself.

"If you'd kept the car your husband bought you—"

"Ex-husband," Lainey said through clenched teeth.

Unperturbed, Jacqui continued on. "If you'd

kept the car, and the husband, you wouldn't need strange men to help you in the parking lot. Men who may have less than honorable intentions toward you."

Lainey tried to count to ten and gave up at three. "Excuse me? How does being nice equal intentions of any kind?"

Jacqui glared at her. "Do I need to spell it out for you? Your father's political connections are extremely valuable. Some people will use you for them. You don't always have the best judgment, Lainey."

Ouch. Direct hit. "Like Daniel did?" Lainey shot back. "You weren't concerned then, about my judgment *or* my connections, since he came from the right family. I can't see what need Ben Lawless would have for political connections, or how he thinks he'd get them when we only had ten minutes together."

"Martha said you looked awful cozy."

"Martha was wrong," Lainey said flatly. "Trust me, Mother. Please."

Jacqui made a noise in her throat. "I talked to Daniel earlier."

Betrayal sliced through her, sharp and quick. "What?"

Jacqui sent Lainey a look full of reproach. "He said you never call him. Why ever not, Lainey? He's a good man."

Lainey sucked in a breath. She'd worked so hard to get free of her ex-husband. "I can't think of any reason I'd ever have to call him." Not even if hell froze over. Twice.

Her mother looked at her as if she were a bit daft. "He misses you, dear."

Not a chance. She knew Daniel. Her ex-husband missed the perceived gravy train.

Lainey had never filled her family in on all the reasons behind her divorce. She'd been afraid they would take his side—a fear only reinforced as she looked at her mother now. Her parents adored Daniel. She'd dated him in an effort to be the daughter they wanted. They'd been over the moon when she'd succumbed in a weak moment, perhaps blinded by the three-carat princess-cut ring, and agreed to marry him. She'd thought she could make it work and earn her parents' respect in one fell swoop.

She'd been wrong.

"Why would he miss me now? We've been divorced more than a year," she said, and wasn't totally successful at keeping the bitterness out of her voice. Jacqui didn't seem to notice.

"I gave him your cell phone number and I've got his for you," she said, fishing in her bag. "He said he'd give you a call."

Anger propelled Lainey to her feet. "What? Mother, how *could* you? I don't want to talk to him. Ever. My life is none of his business now." He'd never cared when they were married. Why would he now?

Surprise crossed her mother's face. "Lainey, you were married for seven years. Those feelings don't just go away. He can help you out of this mess you're in. You're barely hanging on. Everyone knows it. You need his help."

Nausea rolled over Lainey. There lay the crux of the matter for Jacqui—the possibility of another public shaming by her wayward daughter and the offer of salvation by a man deemed worthy, no matter the cost.

"I most certainly do not." Telling her parents the truth of her marriage to Daniel would only prove how good she was at failing. "I don't need him or anyone else to make this work. I'm doing perfectly fine on my own." Well, except for the fact her shop was in the red and she had a cooler and a van on the fritz. Oh, and she was about to become a single mom. Still... "I'm happy, Mother."

Jacqui sighed, shook her head, and gestured around the apartment. "Oh, honey. You can't possibly be happy living like this, after how you were raised and how well you married. Talk to him when he calls. Maybe you'll get lucky and he'll give you a second chance."

Lainey shuddered. God help her. "I'm not interested." Those years she'd spent with Daniel were ones she'd never get back. She wasn't going to repeat the mistake of chaining herself to a man. No matter what.

"You should be." Jacqui glanced at her watch. "I'd better get going. Lovely to see you, dear. Come visit us soon."

Lainey bit back a sigh. Typical. Her mother would act as if nothing had happened. "I'll walk you out."

The next evening Ben looked up at the crunch of tires on the gravel drive. He recognized the silver car, and he already knew Lainey Keeler was coming over to visit his grandmother.

He wondered again at her modest choice of car. Somehow that intrigued him. He'd bet there was more to that story than she'd let on.

It would be flat-out rude not to make sure the car was running okay after he'd helped her yesterday. He'd be polite, then get back to his prep for the wheelchair ramp. He leaned the piece of wood he'd been about to cut against the wall and walked out into the twilight.

As he approached the car the door opened and he watched as Lainey planted one slim denim-clad leg, ending in a high-heeled black boot, on the ground. He tried not to notice how long that leg was. She appeared to be struggling with something so he went over to help.

"Evening," he said. She jumped, yelped, and nearly lost her grip on what he could now see was a pizza box. Big blue eyes swung his way and a pretty pink stained her cheeks. Her lips parted slightly and his gaze zeroed in on her mouth. *Very nice.* He shoved the unwelcome thought away. "Can I get that for you?"

She shook her head and her long hair shifted silkily on her shoulders. "I've got it. Thanks."

He stepped back to let her exit the car. "Is it running okay?"

She glanced up at him. "Yes. Thank you again." Her tone was cool, polite. She bumped the door shut with her hip, but her keys fell to the ground. Ben bent and retrieved them for her, pressing them into her palm. A quick zing of heat flashed through him at the contact. He pulled back quickly. *Hell.*

"Um, thanks," she murmured.

"You're welcome." He turned toward the garage. He needed to get away from her before he started to *feel.*

"Ben." Her voice—hesitant, a little husky—flowed over him. He turned back and she tipped the pizza box slightly toward him. "There's plenty here if you want to join us."

"No, thanks." The words came swift, automatic, but he caught a flash of hurt in her eyes. *Damn it.* "I'm in the middle of a project," he amended. "I'll try and grab some in awhile." Why did he feel the need to soften the blow? Since when had big blue eyes affected him? Since last night, when she'd narrowed her eyes and told him she could change a tire.

She shrugged. "Good luck. Rose and I love our pizza."

He slid his hands in his front pockets. "I'll keep that in mind."

She turned to go and he couldn't tear his gaze off the sway of her hips as she walked up to the house.

Double hell. He couldn't risk forging any type of connection. No way would he allow himself the luxury. How could he, when he shouldn't be the one alive?

Turning, he headed back to his project, tried to ignore the feminine laughter floating through the kitchen's screen door. Lainey's throaty laugh carried, teasing at the edge of something he'd shut down after Jason's death.

His phone rang before he could start the saw. A glance at the display revealed the caller to be his boss. Nerves jolted through him, but he kept his voice steady as he answered.

"Hi, Captain."

"Ben." The concern in the older man's voice carried clearly and Ben shut his eyes against the guilt it stirred up. "How are you, son?"

"I'm getting by," he replied.

"Just getting by?"

"Pretty much." Ben paused. He didn't need to paint a rosy picture for his boss. He'd already been ordered to take leave due to the stress of Jason's death. It couldn't really get any worse than that.

"Still having the symptoms, I take it." Not a question.

"Yeah." When the dream stopped, would he be free of the pain? Did he want to be? Wouldn't that be disloyal to the friend he'd loved like a brother?

After all, Ben was alive. Jason wasn't.

The Captain sighed. "It won't do any good for me to tell you again that it was an accident and not your fault, right?"

"With all due respect, sir, you're wrong." The words caught in Ben's throat. "It was my call. I made a bad one, and a good man—a family man—died because of me."

"That's not what the investigation found," the Captain reminded him softly.

It didn't matter. The investigators hadn't been there—in the inferno, in the moment. "I don't give a damn." Ben shut his eyes against the waves of guilt and pain that buffeted his soul, tried not to see Callie's grief-ravaged face. "I know what happened."

"Ben—"

"Please, don't."

There was a pause, then another sigh. "Then I won't. This time. Son, when you heal, come back and see us. There will always be room for fine firefighters such as yourself and I'd be honored to have you."

Heal. Ben swallowed a lump in his throat. He didn't know if it was possible. "Thank you, sir. I'll keep it in mind."

He disconnected the call and the emptiness he'd been battling for the past six months constricted his chest. He could never work as a firefighter again. He no longer trusted his judgment, his ability to read a situation and respond appropriately.

Without those skills he was nothing.

"Ben?"

He looked up sharply, feeling exposed. Lainey stood in the open door with a plate, uncertainty on her beautiful face. He cursed silently. How much had she overheard?

"Rose thought you might be hungry." She lifted the plate slightly.

He rubbed his hand over his face, afraid the rawness of his emotions showed too clearly. He needed to get them back under control—fast. "Thanks." He shoved the phone in his pocket and walked over, not wanting to look at her and see pity. Or disgust. He'd seen plenty of both over the past couple of months. She handed him the plate wordlessly, then laid her hand on his forearm before he could move away.

His muscles turned to stone even as the heat from her simple touch sought the frozen place inside him. His gaze landed on hers, despite his best intent. He saw no pity, only questions, and he couldn't take the chance of her asking them. Not now, with everything so close to the surface.

He cleared his throat and she stepped back quickly, taking her warmth with her when she removed her hand. It was a much sharper loss than he'd like. "Thanks for the pizza."

"Sure." She hesitated and he held his breath, afraid she'd ask. Perversely, he was almost afraid she wouldn't. She gave him a small smile. "Eat it before it gets cold."

Then she turned and walked into the night before he could tell her how very familiar he was with cold.

And what a lonely place it was.

CHAPTER THREE

AN IMPERIAL SUMMONS was never a good thing.

Lainey had long thought of her mother's invitations to dinner as such a summons—and more often than not they included some well-meaning but completely off-base idea of her parents' to "improve her life."

She'd met her ex at such a dinner. And apparently she was the only one who saw it for the farce it had turned out to be.

Now, if Daniel had been a man like Ben maybe things would have been different. The thought wasn't as shocking as it might have been, considering she'd been unable to get Ben and the haunted look on his face out of her mind for the past two days. She hadn't overheard enough of his conversation to find out what was eating him alive, but she'd heard the pain layering his voice, each word laced with more than the last.

Still, Ben struck her as a fundamentally honorable man, not one who would marry for money without dumping his long-time girlfriend first. Like, say, her ex-husband. The good thing was her heart hadn't been involved—but her pride and self-worth had taken a beating.

Lainey sighed and turned through the thick stone columns into her parents' driveway. Since her parents were expecting her, the black iron gate stood open. She wound her way up the drive and parked in front of the massive log house that managed to be both rustic and majestic.

Lainey turned the car off and got out. On the plus side Grace, the cook, always put together fabulous meals, so she'd make sure she enjoyed that even while avoiding the bombs that were likely to be lobbed over the table. The front door opened even before she made it all the way up the carefully landscaped walkway.

"Lainey!" her father greeted her in his big voice.

"Hi, Dad." She allowed herself to be drawn into a hug. Tall and trim, Greg Keeler cut a handsome picture with his dark, youthful looks, a perfect foil to Jacqui's petite blond paleness. Even in their late fifties, they looked every inch the power couple they'd been for as long as she could remember.

"Come on in. We're in the family room."

He turned and Lainey followed him into the large room off the foyer, with its high ceilings, thick carpet and fireplace. While the outside screamed North Woods, inside the only concession to the house's rustic roots were the thick beams soaring overhead.

Lainey walked across the luxurious carpet, its velvety pile the color of cream, with nary a stain in sight. She tried to picture a baby crawling around in here and failed. Nothing about this room said *family*—even with the professionally shot family photos on the mantel. She vowed to make sure she raised her baby in an environment that was warm and welcoming, not precious and impersonal.

Her mother perched on the edge of a chair near the fire. A manila folder lay on an end table next to her.

"Hello, dear." Jacqui rose and offered her cheek to Lainey, who came around the end of the sofa to place the obligatory kiss.

"Hi, Mother."

"Have a seat." Her dad gestured toward the sofa and turned to the mini-wet-bar. "Can I get you anything to drink?"

Well, no. I'm pregnant. She swallowed the words. That would get this little pow-wow off to a roaring start. In fact it might create stains on the carpet from dropped or flying liquor. "No, thanks."

He raised an eyebrow but said nothing as he mixed his drink quickly and took the seat opposite Jacqui.

Lainey flicked her gaze between both of them. There was no reading her parents. Whatever they'd done, they wouldn't be smug, since they'd consider it a necessary move. She might as well get it over with. "What's going on?"

Jacqui frowned a little. "Wouldn't you rather eat first? Grace has a lovely roast chicken prepared."

Lainey's shoulders tensed at the deflection. "I'd like to know what's going on." She looked at her father but his expression was unreadable. "Dad? Please?"

He down set his drink—a screwdriver, no

doubt. "Might as well cut to the chase. Lainey, we want to help you."

Oh, no. Her stomach lurched. She threaded her fingers together in her lap to keep from shaking. She kept her tone measured. "Help me how?"

"With your little shop, honey." Jacqui reached for the folder and the hairs went up on the back of Lainey's neck.

"My little shop? What have you done, Mother? Dad?" She heard the note of panic in her voice. She'd been safe, had rented the business from Esther Browning, what could they possibly—?

Jacqui beamed. "We thought you'd be pleased to know we bought your building."

The room tilted a little and Lainey gripped the arm of the chair, struggling to focus on her mother's clueless face. She couldn't have heard correctly. "I'm sorry—what? Why?"

"You're having such a hard time getting this going, and Esther was worried about making ends meet. You know she needs the rent to live on, dear."

My parents are now my landlords. The realization swept through her, followed closely by rage. "I've never paid late. Not one single payment."

She bit off each word. If nothing else, she prided herself on that. She knew her elderly landlord depended on that income, and made absolutely sure those payments went out on time.

Her father cut in. "Of course not. But there's reason to believe you might have a hard time making them, so we thought this would help both of you out."

Lainey sucked in a breath. Poor Esther. The prospect of having the building all paid for, most likely in cash, must have been powerful. She'd done what was best for her, and Lainey refused to fault her for that.

Keeping her voice even, she asked, "But you didn't think maybe you should ask me? See how I'm doing?" Of course the documents would have been anything but reassuring, but still… Betrayal rose in her throat, the taste bitter, and she swallowed hard. Why was it too much for them to think to include her in the decision making?

Jacqui looked surprised. Or would have if the Botox hadn't been working so well. "Well, we already know how you're doing. The whole town does. We've got your best interests at heart, dear. Always."

Lainey shut her eyes. How often had she heard that little line? When would it actually prove to be true? "How exactly does this help me?" She braced herself for the kicker.

"Well, you won't have the monthly payment anymore. We won't make you pay rent. And you can live here now. We'll rent out that little apartment." Her mother sounded pleased, as if she'd truly solved a problem. Her father nodded in agreement as they exchanged a look.

She sucked in a sharp breath. "No. I can't live here." *How am I supposed to puke in private every morning? Hide my rounding belly? Raise my child here?* Panic seized her and she jumped up as her father's phone rang. He checked it, and rose.

"I've got to run. Lainey, we'll talk more later. But for now we feel this is the best thing for you."

He kissed her cheek and strode out of the room. Lainey stared after him, floored because both of her parents seemed to think this was a done deal and hadn't bothered to truly consider *her*. "Why did no one ask me? Has no one noticed I'm an adult? I'm not moving back home." Where she'd go, she didn't know. But it wouldn't be here.

Jacqui set her snifter on the table. "Of course you are, dear. That little place isn't good for you. We've got plenty of room. We can remodel your suite if you'd like. Daniel agrees you should be here."

Lainey whipped around so fast she nearly got dizzy. "He has no say in my life. None. We're divorced, remember?"

Jacqui leaned forward, her gaze earnest. "You were wrong, Lainey. He loves you and he's willing to give you a second chance. What is so bad about that? Now you don't have to struggle anymore. We've taken care of it."

Lainey stared back. Her mother really believed it. She could see the sincerity in the other woman's gaze, hear it in her voice. They didn't understand it was Lainey's problem and she wanted to be the one to solve it—or not. That had been the whole point of taking over the shop—to make it work by herself. Now the choice was gone.

She lifted her chin and met her mother's expectant gaze. "I'm not coming home." Each word came out crystal-clear and Jacqui's eyes widened. "I'm happy where I am. I love my job, my shop. My apartment. I'm not going to give it up, give you control of my life, because you can't accept I'm an adult and haven't chosen the path or the man you wanted for me."

Jacqui frowned. "Lainey, please be reasonable. You needed help. We gave it to you."

"Yes, but at what cost to *me*?" Despair rose and Lainey fought it back, preferring anger. There was really only one option here, since she wasn't going to walk away from the shop she loved. "What do I have to do to get it back?"

Jacqui sat back. "Pardon?"

"I want it back," she repeated. "I'll buy the building flat out from you. And you'll have to completely butt out of my life."

Jacqui frowned, as if this wasn't going the way she'd planned. "I don't think—"

Lainey stood up, the words she should have said years ago boiling out of her. "I'm not letting you force me into this. And there's no hope for Daniel. You have no idea what my marriage was like. *None.* I'd hope you'd want better for me, even if it's not what you would have chosen." She picked up her purse with shaking hands. "I'm going, Mother. I'll find somewhere else to live. And don't worry. I will make those rent payments on my shop. They will be on time. I'm never late."

Pulse roaring in her ears, she walked away before Jacqui could say anything else.

The nerve. Lainey pulled over a couple of miles past the house and sat for a minute, tears of rage pouring down her face. *The nerve.*

Poor Esther. Lainey hoped they'd at least given the woman a fair price. But while apparently not above blackmail, her parents weren't cheats. One small thing in this whole mess to take comfort in.

What she needed was a plan. One that could get her the money, and the time, to solve this herself—which was all she wanted. Just to prove she could do it—run a business, be successful on her own terms without any help from her family.

To show them she wasn't a screw-up, but just as worthy of being a Keeler as they were.

She fished a napkin out of the glove box and wiped her face. Crying wasn't going to solve anything. She put the car back in gear and headed for the public park at the lake. She'd spent many hours here as a kid, and later as a teen when she'd needed space. Sure, there was a private beach at her parents' home, but the park had swings and a playground, now upgraded to a fancy plastic playscape. They'd kept the old metal merry-go-round, her favorite thing in the park.

The gathering twilight and chilly breeze off the water ensured the park itself was empty, though a couple cars parked nearby indicated joggers still out on the loop that ran next to the water.

Lainey pulled the hood of her jacket up and settled on a swing. She scuffed her feet in the wood chips, then backed up, ready to swing. Back and forth she went, pumping her legs, stretching out in the swing until her hood slid off and her hair fell in her face when she leaned forward. The moon hung over the quiet lake, full and incandescent, a bright star to its left. *Star light, star bright, first star I see tonight.* A small laugh escaped her, followed by more tears. She'd gone way beyond childish wishes, even if as a kid she'd believed in the power of the first star. The tensions of her parents' betrayal slid away in the stinging wind, into the encroaching darkness. Finally she stopped pumping, let herself glide through the cool evening air, slowly coming to a stop.

A motion to her left caught her eye and she turned her head.

Ben Lawless sat on the merry-go-round, watching her. Her belly clutched. Oh, no. What was he doing here?

"Did it work?" Despite his low tone, she heard him clearly.

Caught, Lainey forced herself to meet his gaze. "Did what work?"

"The swinging. The tears. You looked like you were trying to get rid of something."

She tilted her head so it rested on the chain. No point in denying it. She didn't want to. "For the moment, maybe." Though the ache under her heart hadn't gone away.

Her parents had bought her building. She squeezed her eyes shut as another wave of betrayal washed over her. How had she not seen it coming?

When she looked back over at Ben he stood up from the merry-go-round, gave it a small shove with his hand. It wobbled in a slow circle. "For the moment?"

Lainey scuffed her foot in the wood chips. Was that an opening for her to talk, no matter how reluctantly issued? She almost laughed. Where would she start? With her parents? With her baby? With her ex-husband? With the father of said baby? "I don't know. Can we not talk about it?" The very thought of trying to explain the twisted mess her life had become exhausted her.

Ben laughed—a quick deep flash that sent tingles though her body. "As long as we don't talk about me."

His grief-stricken face flashed across her memory. "Deal." She hopped out of the swing and her balance shifted a bit. No doubt an effect of her pregnancy. She started toward the water, simply needing to move.

She was surprised when Ben caught up to her. He walked beside her, his arm almost brushing hers. Even without the contact she could feel the heat from his big body as hers seemed to be *way* too tuned in to him.

This was bad.

Distracted, she stumbled a bit on the uneven sand. He caught her arm—pure reflex, she was sure—especially because he let go of her almost as soon as he touched her, as though she'd burned him somehow.

"Careful," he said, his voice low.

"Thanks," she murmured, keeping her eyes on the ground. His scent, a yummy mix of soap and fresh air, drifted over to her. She curled her fingers into fists and shoved them in her pockets so she didn't do something stupid—like reach for him and bury her face in his chest.

Even as the urge confused and scared her she knew Ben wouldn't lie to her, use her, or treat her like a wayward child. Even with his secrets, he came across as sincere in a way she so wanted to believe in.

Except she was done with believing.

They stopped when they reached the lake. The water was almost mirror-still. Perfect for skipping rocks. When was the last time she'd done that? The moon was bright enough that she could see pretty well, so she started to hunt for flat stones. She didn't look at Ben, but could feel him watching her.

Strangely, not talking felt right. She didn't feel she needed to fill the night with chatter—after the bombshell her parents had laid on her that was a good thing—and he seemed to be quiet because he was more comfortable without words.

She picked up a rock—a flat disk, smooth and cold in her hand. She lined up and let it fly over the still water, counting twelve skips. She couldn't resist a little fist pump. She still had it after all these years.

"Not bad." Ben fingered his own rock. "My turn."

"Good luck," she said politely. She'd always been a top-notch rock-skipper. One of her many under-appreciated talents. She couldn't smother a small sigh. No doubt her mother would be appalled.

His rock flew over the water. Thirteen skips.

"Hmm." Glad for the distraction, Lainey narrowed her eyes when he turned to her, eyebrow raised. "I can beat that."

A small laugh escaped him and he looked surprised at the sound. Her heart tugged. Had he really gone so long in sorrow he'd lost laughter?

He leaned toward her, not close enough to touch, but close enough to see the challenge in his eyes. "You're on."

His warm breath feathered over her cheek and her little shiver had nothing to do with the chill in the air. "Good luck," she said again. The words came out a little husky, and she turned away quickly to look for more rocks. What was wrong with her? What was it about Ben Lawless that drew her in? It was wrong on so many levels. She was pregnant, for God's sake. And her life was a mess. There was no room for a man. Especially one with issues of his own.

It took everything Ben had not to ask why she'd been crying. The tracks from her tears were dry now, but even in the light of the moon he could see her beautiful blue eyes were red-rimmed. An unwelcome protective surge caught him off-guard and left a sour feeling in his stomach.

He couldn't protect anyone. He knew that. But tonight he'd been drawn in by her obvious distress. Since she was a friend of his grandma's it had seemed wrong just to walk away until he knew she was okay.

Yeah, that was all it was. A favor to Grandma. *Riiiight...*

Choosing to ignore his inner voice, he let his gaze follow her as she searched for rocks along the water's edge. The moon's light turned her hair to silver as she lifted potential candidates, weighed them in her hand, then discarded some and slipped others into her pockets. That unfamiliar smile tugged at his mouth. She took this seriously. He'd do the same.

He picked up a few rocks of his own and was ready when she came back. Determination sparked in her eyes. He swallowed hard. "You ready?" If she noticed the rasp in his voice she didn't show it.

"I'm ready. I'll go first."

She stepped forward to the edge of the water and Ben allowed himself to admire her slender figure as she let the rock fly and stood, as if she were holding her breath, until it sank, leaving an expanding ring of ripples on the water's surface.

"Ten skips."

"Not bad." He moved up next to her. "But let me show you how it's done."

He was rewarded with an eye-roll. He bit back another grin.

He took his turn and after nine skips she turned to him, her glee barely contained. "*That's* how it's done?"

In spite of himself he laughed again, the feeling foreign after so many months of not being able to. It felt—good. But scary, too. Here in the moonlight, with a beautiful woman who wanted nothing from him, playing a silly game, he was almost relaxed.

Back and forth they went, and after six stones each Ben sent her a look. "This is it. Winner takes all."

She arched a brow and pulled out her final stone. "Really? What does the winner get?"

"Bragging rights."

"Good enough." She pulled out her final stone and readied herself. She let it fly and Ben watched it, counting the skips until it sank.

"Fifteen skips." Triumph filled her voice. "Beat that, Ben."

He took his turn and they both watched as his rock sank after twelve. "You win."

She did another fist-pump. "Yay. I like to win." Then frowned. "No offense."

He shook his head. "None taken." He hesitated. "Better?"

She nodded, but he saw the shadow that fell over her features. "Yes. Thank you for staying."

He turned with her to walk back. "No problem. You're my grandma's friend."

There was the tiniest of hitches in her step. "Right. Of course."

He forced himself to ignore the hurt in her tone. He needed to build the distance between them back up. But when she turned those big blue eyes on him something long buried inside him cracked. "Lainey—"

She gave a little shake of her head as she reached her car. "Thanks again."

To hell with it.

Ben turned her around as she fumbled in her pocket for her keys. Her eyes widened and her lips parted, but before she could say anything he dipped his head and covered her mouth with his.

After a heartbeat her cold mouth opened and let him into her warmth. God, it had been so long since he'd felt anything, *anything*, and she was warm and soft and so, so sweet. He fisted his hand in her hair, to angle her head so he could go deeper, and her moan lit fires inside him that had long been dormant.

For a reason.

He broke the kiss and stepped back, his ragged breath catching in his chest. God, what had he done?

She blinked up at him, her gaze smoky and

slightly confused. Then her eyes cleared and a look of pure horror crossed her face.

"I've got to go," she said, yanking her keys out of her pocket.

"Lainey, I'm sorry." As soon as the words were out he knew they were the wrong thing to say.

Her back stiffened as she unlocked the car. "It's forgotten." She got in the car and slammed the door.

He stood in the cold and cursed as her taillights disappeared out of the park. Hell. He'd just made a huge mess of something he had no right even to start.

And he had no idea how to fix it.

CHAPTER FOUR

"THEY DID WHAT?" Beth's words ended on a small shriek. The look on her face would have been comical if Lainey could muster the energy to laugh. "No way. Is that even legal?"

"Unfortunately," Lainey said as she selected a few silk 'mums for the centerpiece she was working on.

"They're kicking you out," Beth breathed. "I never thought—"

"It's not technically a kick out," Lainey corrected her. "It's a very strong suggestion I move in with them." And a heck of a way to do it, too. Though where in the budget she'd find the money to rent a place plus continue to pay her parents she didn't know.

How had it not occurred to her parents that their "helping" would put her in this kind of bind?

Beth frowned. "Are you going to? How would that work with the baby?"

A chill ran through Lainey. "I can't think of anything I want less than to live there. Especially since my mother is apparently in cahoots with Daniel. I'm going to ask Rose if she knows of any rental houses. I know she owns a couple."

Maybe she'd get lucky and one would be open. On the other hand, that would make Rose her landlord, and she wasn't sure she wanted to risk extra contact with Ben. The kiss flashed through her mind and a delicious little shiver ran through her. It had been a mistake, which he'd acknowledged. She had to agree. But a small part of her was hurt. She'd spent much of her adult life being made to feel everything she did was a mistake. To hear it after something as sweet as that kiss, on top of her parents' antics, had cut deep.

"Wow." Beth shook her head and cut a length of ribbon. "I'm just floored."

"Yeah, me too." Lainey fitted the 'mums into the floral foam and stepped back. "These look nice. Let's get them in the window."

It took a nice chunk of time to redo the front windows with a fall theme geared toward Halloween. Lainey was pleased with the result. She glanced at the clock. Almost noon. "I need to call Jon and tell him."

Beth came around the counter. "Do you need me there?"

Lainey gave her friend a hug. "Thanks, but, no. I'll be fine. I just need to get it over with."

She climbed the stairs to her apartment with butterflies roiling in her stomach. She and Jon hadn't even bothered to exchange contact info. It had been pretty clear how forgettable the whole thing was—or would have been except for the baby.

Her hands shook as she sat down at the computer and pulled up the website she'd found for Jon's company. Since California was three hours behind Michigan it was early morning there, so she hoped she had a chance of catching him at his office.

It took two tries to dial the number correctly, but amazingly she got through. His assistant sounded about twenty and possessive, and Lainey bet Jon valued looks over work ethic. How could she have such poor judgment when it came to men?

"Jon Meier." His crisp voice sent a chill over her skin.

"It's Lainey Keeler. We—ah—met at the reunion." She stumbled a bit over the words. How exactly did one phrase *one-night stand* for polite company?

A pause. "Lainey. What's going on?" His tone was wary.

Lainey stared at the ceiling of her living room. It seemed there was only one thing to say and one way to say it. "I'm pregnant."

The silence roared in her ears. She gripped the small phone tighter.

"Jon?" she ventured after a few seconds.

"I'm here," he said, sounding slightly strangled. "Are you sure it's mine?"

Indignation spiked. "Of course it's yours. Who else's would it be?" Like she was some slut.

He said a clear and succinct curse word and Lainey winced.

"I'm sorry," he said, his voice low. "But there's something you should know."

Her heart kicked up in a pattern of dread. Those words never meant anything good. "What's that?"

She heard him exhale roughly. "I'm married."

Nausea hit Lainey like a freight train. Oh, God. *Married?* How had she not known? He was just like her ex-husband. Her stomach rolled and she sank down on the floor, hand pressed over her mouth. *Oh, no. No, no.*

"Lainey? Are you still there?"

I'm married. The words almost physically crawled over her skin. She'd played a role in the betrayal of a marriage. *What Daniel did to me.*

"Oh, my God. How could you? You cheated on your wife." She couldn't keep the horror and disgust out of her voice.

There was a rustle of paper. "Well, in my admittedly weak defense, we were going through a rough patch. She doesn't—she doesn't know. I can't have her know. I can pay to take care of it, though, if you'd rather not have it."

It took her a second to sort through the numerous atrocities in those sentences. "Are you—are you offering to pay for an abortion?"

"You're what? Eight weeks? Early enough. Listen, Lainey—"

"No." The word came out furious and flat. Temper rose like bile in her throat, a sharp burn.

"I can't be a father to that baby, Lainey. My wife—she's pregnant, too. I can't risk—"

"Can't risk what? Her finding out what a slime you are?" She couldn't help the angry words. Not because she wanted him in her life, or the baby's, but because she'd given her child this kind of man for a father. The same kind of man her ex was. She pressed her hand over her eyes, willing the tears of anger and frustration away.

He let out a sigh. "Something like that. Listen, I haven't been the best husband, okay? I get that. But we are finally getting on the right track again. I can't—I just can't risk it."

Lainey sucked in a breath. The depth of his deception hit her hard. She couldn't get involved in his mess, though. She and her baby would stay above this.

She couldn't keep the disgust out of her voice. "I want you to sign off on all parental rights. I don't want you in my child's life."

"I'll talk to my lawyers," he said after a moment, and she allowed herself to breathe again. "I don't see how I could be involved even if I wanted to be. My wife..." His voice trailed off.

Then, "I'm sorry, Lainey. I really am. But—you understand?"

Your poor wife. Lainey truly felt for her. She could see her own ex-husband pulling this exact same stunt. For all she knew he had. The thought made her even angrier. "What I understand is you are a cheating, lying bastard. When will I hear from you?"

"End of the week," he said, apparently unfazed by her description of him. "I'll need your contact info. I'd prefer to communicate through email, if we need to discuss anything further."

"Fine with me." She gave him the relevant information and hung up, mind whirling. The sick feeling wouldn't recede. Most likely she'd get what she wanted, but at what cost? What could she tell her baby? The loss here was truly Jon's, but her baby deserved a father.

She dropped her face into her hands. Given her track record with men who seemed great on the surface but were total losers, she wasn't sure she could trust herself to know a good man when she met him. She pushed herself off the floor and went to get a glass of water.

Ben flashed across her mind. He was a good

man. His kiss. His quiet playfulness last night. Even though it had seemed as if he was coming out of a deep shell, for that scant hour she'd spent with him he'd been more real than her husband or Jon had ever been. Maybe it was because he hadn't wanted anything from her. Maybe it had to do with the other two men being cheaters. Another wave of nausea flowed over her and she put her head back in her hands. She'd been with a married man. How had she not known? How could she know, with no ring and no mention of a wife?

She went back downstairs. A couple of months ago her life had been pretty simple. Keep her shop open and stay out of her parents' line of fire. Period. Now she was looking at single motherhood and her parents buying their way into her life and pulling her ex along—not to mention her odd connection to Ben.

Maybe one of these days she'd do something the easy way, instead of somehow making everything as difficult as possible.

Lainey called Rose that evening and at her friend's invitation went over to her house. She didn't want to see Ben, seeing as how the awkwardness level there would be epic, but she wasn't going to avoid her friend. Plus, being with someone who didn't want to manipulate her sounded wonderful.

She didn't see Ben's truck, which was both a relief and an unexpected disappointment. Ignoring the disappointment part, she saw he'd been busy. The framework for the ramp was already in place. It touched a little sweet spot in her that he took his grandma's issues so seriously.

Rose opened the kitchen door with a concerned look. "Hi, honey. Come on in. Everything okay?"

She stepped in with a smile. "Yes. Just a little tired." She didn't ask where Ben was as she slipped her jacket off. She told herself she didn't care. Not to mention it was very important that Rose did not realize Lainey's conflicted emotions regarding Ben. She didn't want any matchmaking attempts, and she doubted Ben would appreciate it, either. Possibly less than she did, if his aloof manner was any indication.

But, oh, the man could kiss.

"Dear, you look a little flushed. Are you sure you're okay?" Rose wheeled over to the table.

Her face heated even more. She couldn't very well tell the older woman she'd kissed her grandson, so she took a seat at the table and filled Rose in on her parents' bombshell.

Rose frowned when she'd finished. "I'm sorry, Lainey. I understand they mean well, or think they do, but they really don't take you into consideration, do they?"

Lainey stared at the table, a small knot in her throat. It was the truth. "Not really."

Rose reached over and squeezed her hand. "Well, as it happens I've got a little place you can rent." Her surprise must have shown on her face because Rose chuckled. "I do. I've got a little rental house over by the lake. The same couple has rented it for—oh, goodness—decades. Thirty years or so? Anyway, they moved out a couple weeks ago. Decided to retire in Florida."

Lainey opened her mouth, then closed it. Hope surged through her. "I—wow. Really?"

"Of course. Two bedrooms. Nice backyard. It's a little Cape Cod. Not real large, but plenty big for you and your cat."

Relief rushed through her. "It sounds wonderful."

Rose reached for the phone. "It needs a little

work. Nothing major. Just some freshening up and some minor repairs. Why don't you go take a look? Ben's over there now, assessing what all needs to be done. He seemed to think it could be ready in around a week or so. You can even pick your paint colors."

Ben was there. Anticipation zipped through her, too quick for her to stifle. She didn't see a way to refuse without raising Rose's suspicions. "All right. I'd love to see it, if you're sure?"

Rose waved a hand. "Of course I'm sure. I can't think of anyone I'd like more to have for a tenant than you. Let me call him real quick and you can head over."

Lainey followed Rose's directions to the house, which was on the other side of the lake from her parents' place, a block from the water. The little white house was charming, from what she could see as she pulled in the driveway behind Ben's truck. It had a garage, a front porch, and the backyard was fenced. A little shiver of excitement ran though her.

"It's very cute," she said aloud as she walked up

to the front porch. The light was on. She knocked, then stuck her head in. "Hello?"

She'd been hoping somehow that Ben wouldn't be here, or that someone else would be here, too. Anything but just the two of them. Not that she couldn't control herself—of course she could— it was just the last thing she needed was another complication in her life. As Ben appeared in the living room archway she couldn't help but wish all complications could be so hot.

"Lainey?" Ben said, looking behind her. "I'm sorry. Grandma said there was a potential tenant coming to check the place out."

In spite of her nerves, Lainey laughed. *Oh, Rose.* "It's me. I'm the tenant."

"You?" His brow shot up. "I thought you lived above your shop."

Lainey closed the door behind her and un-zipped her jacket. She couldn't quite keep her voice steady. "Not for long."

She saw understanding dawn in his eyes, but all he said was, "I see."

Awareness sparked between them, hot and deep, and she knew while he didn't mention it he was thinking about *the kiss*. Lainey pulled her gaze off him and focused on the wall behind him. He looked so good, even with the wary expression he seemed to wear perpetually. Except the other night, when he'd actually laughed. And kissed her.

Darn it. She shut her eyes. *Not helpful.*

"You okay?"

She opened them again and gave him a small smile. "Peachy." She gestured with her hand. "Can I look around?"

Ben stepped back out of the doorway. "Sure. Kitchen—dining room through there—" he pointed to his right "—bedrooms. Bathroom that way. I'll be in the kitchen if you need anything." Then he disappeared.

She took a minute to wander around the room she stood in—a good-sized living room, with two large windows and a fireplace, flanked by two smaller, higher windows over built-in bookcases. The former tenants' drapes remained, but otherwise the room was bare. The floor was hardwood, scuffed and worn and in need of being redone. She rubbed the toe of her shoe on it. How would a hard floor be with a baby? Maybe she could get some thick rugs. The paint color was an odd shade of pinkish tan, but maybe that was the light from the overhead fixture, which was a little harsh. Still, it had charm and lots of potential.

She walked across the floor and it creaked under her feet. She heard banging and swearing from the direction of the kitchen, so she detoured that way down the short hall.

Ben was on his knees, bent over, half in the cabinet under the sink, and her gaze locked on his very fine butt and flexed thigh muscles. The back of his shirt had ridden up, exposing an inch or so of an equally nice back. She blinked and forced herself to refocus.

"Is there a problem?" she asked.

He scrambled back out from the cabinet, whacked his head and muttered another choice word. She winced.

"Sorry," she said. "Are you okay?"

"Fine." He stood up and rubbed the back of his head. "Need something?"

"Um…no. I heard some noise and thought I'd see what was going on in here." She looked at the array of tools and wet towels on the floor. "Maybe you need a plumber?"

Ben stared at her, then let out a sharp bark of laughter. "What I need is another wrench." He bent over and she tried very hard to keep her eyes off his butt and failed. She very much wanted to chalk it up to pregnancy hormones, except for the little fact she wasn't attracted to any other man but this one. He pulled out two pieces of what had been a wrench and held them up.

"Oh. That's not good."

"No kidding. Are you parked behind me?"

He was going right now? The little stab she felt couldn't be disappointment. It had to be relief. "Yes. I'll move my car."

He turned away to wipe his hands on the towel lying on the counter. She glanced around the room, noting the old but serviceable appliances, the Formica counters that were a bit worn, the old linoleum on the floor. The cabinets were in good condition. It was a nice size. It would work well for her.

"Not what you're used to, I'm sure," Ben said and she blinked at him.

"What isn't?"

He swept his hand out, indicating the room. "This."

It took her a second, then anger spiked. "Oh, for God's sake. Why would you think that?"

He just looked at her and she shook her head, sadness chasing the anger away. Just because she'd been raised in a wealthy household it didn't mean those things mattered to her. "You don't know me. At all. I'd appreciate it if you'd keep your judgments to yourself. I'll go move my car to the street."

Ben shut his eyes as she stomped off. He'd achieved his goal, which had been to drive her away, but he felt no sense of victory. Only shame. She'd looked way too hot, standing there in her jeans, boots and sweatshirt, with her hair up in a ponytail. None of it was even particularly form-fitting, but it was enough. Worse, he'd wanted to touch her, to feel her hot, responsive mouth under his again. That was dangerous. *Wanting* was something he tried to keep a lid on, along with feeling. He saw her headlights flash across the wall as she backed out of the driveway.

Now he needed to apologize. Whatever had prompted last night's crying jag had brought her here today, and it wasn't right for him to make it harder for her just because he was attracted to her. Or to lose a tenant for his grandmother.

So he went into the living room and didn't back down under the cold glare she leveled at him when she came through the door. "I'm sorry. I was out of line."

She considered him, her blue eyes cool. Finally she nodded. "You were. But I accept your apology. Next time don't assume you know anything about me."

I know how you kiss, he wanted to tell her. *I know how you feel in my arms, how soft your skin is under my hand. I know how your breasts feel against me.*

She must have read his thoughts on his face because her gaze skittered off his and she jingled her keys in her hand. He cleared his throat, trying to bring his thoughts back around.

"Okay, then. I'm going to go. If you leave before I get back you can lock the door behind you. Also, if you're considering renting this place, start thinking of paint colors. The sooner you can get them to me, the better. I can get started as soon as I finish a few repairs."

She nodded. "I will. I like it. So far I think it'll suit us just fine."

"Let me know." As he escaped out into the night, he wondered, *Who's us?*

CHAPTER FIVE

LAINEY SHUDDERED OUT a deep breath when the door closed behind him. There had been no mistaking the look on his face when she'd said he didn't know her. Odd that he could know her a little physically but not at all as a person.

It seemed to be a pattern. Her ex-husband had never attempted to really get to know her. He'd had his secretary take care of gifts and things. She'd allowed herself to pretend it was because he was busy, but she knew it had been because he'd never cared enough to find out.

Lesson learned.

She shoved all the thoughts away and walked down the hall to the bedrooms. Two of them, both of which were bigger than her bedroom at the apartment, plus a decent-sized bathroom. Another door led to an open and clean attic.

She went back to the kitchen, where she found a small pantry, an entryway by the back door with hooks for coats, and stairs to the basement. A quick scout revealed it to be clean and apparently dry, and she found the laundry hook-ups. At some point the space might make a good play area, if there was a way to cover the cement with carpet.

Back upstairs, she mused over paint colors as she went back to the bedrooms. She hadn't decided yet if she wanted to know if she was having a boy or a girl. Then she frowned. Either way, probably better to go neutral. That way she could forestall any questions for longer.

With a groan, she rested her head on the doorjamb. It wouldn't matter. Her little secret would out itself in a matter of weeks. Her pants were already feeling a little snug, and she had taken to wearing slightly baggy tops to cover up.

That wouldn't work much longer.

Her phone rang and she fished it out of her pocket. Seeing Rose's number, she answered.

"What do you think?" There was excitement in Rose's voice and Lainey had to smile.

"I love it."

"I knew it." The smugness in her friend's tone

made Lainey laugh. "Come on back tomorrow and we'll sign a lease."

Lainey hesitated. "How much are you asking?" She'd told her parents she'd make rent payments anyway, and to add house rent on top of it would seriously stretch her already tight budget even more.

Rose named an amount that Lainey knew had to be way low, considering the size of the house and the location. "Rose, are you sure? That's not much."

"The house is paid for," her friend said, then added impishly, "And don't you dare argue with your elders."

Lainey laughed and flicked the light switch off in what would be the baby's room. "Well, when you put it like that…"

"You can help do some of the work if you want," Rose said. "Painting and such."

"Sure," Lainey said. How would that work with being pregnant? She'd have to make sure it was safe before she cracked open a paint can.

They talked a few more minutes, then Lainey hung up. She locked the door behind her after one last look around. She would make a home here, for herself and her baby. But to get it she'd have to work with Ben.

Ignoring the little thrill that gave her, she started her car. She needed to remember Ben would leave. She was going to be a single mother. He was clearly struggling with some kind of issues of his own. None of that held hope for any kind of relationship.

And the very fact she'd even thought the word *relationship* in regard to Ben was troubling.

"So, I've found a place to live," Lainey told Beth as she carefully unpacked the latest shipment of flowers the next morning.

"Really? That was fast."

"Yep. It was perfect timing. Rose has an empty rental house."

Beth snipped the ends off a handful of lilies before plunging them in the water bucket. "Hmm. Will this put you in contact with her very appealing grandson?"

Lainey's face heated. Of course Beth *would* make that connection. "I wouldn't call him appealing," she hedged. *Liar.* "She wants me to help with the cleaning and painting and stuff. Which Ben is doing."

Beth set her scissors down, arched her brow. "Hmm. Is there something you're not telling me, Lainey?"

Lainey busied herself breaking down an empty box. Then she gave up. Her friend would figure it out anyway. "He kissed me."

Beth's mouth dropped open. "Holy cow! When? Was it amazing?"

Amazing? Lainey recalled the tender yet hot way his mouth had moved over hers and her whole body buzzed. "Um… After the thing with my parents. And, yes, I guess it was."

"You *guess*?" Beth's eyes bugged out. "He doesn't look like the type to rate 'I guess' on the kissing scale."

She had a point. "Okay, yeah, it was amazing."

Beth grinned. "I knew it. So. Spill. What happened?"

Lainey filled her in on her visit to the park and finding Ben there. She finished with, "But it was a mistake. It won't happen again."

Beth shook her head. "Why not?" The front doorbell jingled and she pointed a finger at

Lainey. "Don't go anywhere. We're not done here." Then she hurried out front and Lainey heard her greet the customer.

Lainey's phone buzzed in her pocket and she pulled it out. She didn't recognize the number, but answered anyway, tucking it under her chin as she reached for the next box of flowers. "Hello?"

"Lainey?"

Her blood froze. She'd recognize that smooth voice on the other end of the line anywhere. Flowers forgotten, she gripped the phone so hard it hurt.

"Daniel." His name fell like a razor off her tongue. "What do you want?"

He chuckled—a low sound that sent chills up her spine. How had it ever thrilled her? "Why, to talk to you, baby. It's been a long time. Can't I talk to my wife?"

"Ex-wife," she corrected, because it had been hard-won and it mattered.

"Whatever," he said, and she pictured him waving away her words with a sweep of his hand, like so many pesky flies. "It's just details. Can we get together soon? I'd love to see you."

She nearly dropped the phone as rage rolled

through her. "No. Way. I've got nothing left to say to you." As if he'd ever listened, ever heard her.

"Laine. It's been so long. I miss you. I made a mistake." The seductive tone of his voice made her skin crawl and she shivered.

"Yeah, so did I," she muttered. Her marriage had been one big fat mistake from start to finish.

"Lainey, please." Now he sounded almost pleading.

"No." Oh, it felt so good to tell him that. "I can't talk right now, Daniel. I'm at work."

He sighed. "So I've heard. Some little flower shop, right? It's not going well. Your mother said you're having some problems—"

"Having some problems?" she sputtered. His condescending tone had her teeth grinding together. This was the Daniel she knew. "It's a new business. I'm still getting it off the ground."

"Yes, but it's been—what?—nine months? It was an honest try but it's not getting better, Lainey. You need to face reality."

Hearing him voice her own fears made her stomach churn.

His tone turned slightly wheedling. "I'd love to help. I think we could make it work this time."

"Did she dump you?"

A beat, then, "I'm sorry? Who?"

"You don't want me, Daniel. You never did. You want what you think I stand for. Calling me and belittling my shop and the life I've built without you is not going to change my mind. Nothing will," she qualified. Fueled by her chat with Jon, she added, "You cheated. You used me. Don't call me again."

"Lainey, for God's sake, just listen. You can't do this." His anger snapped through the connection and for a heartbeat she froze.

"I am doing it. Goodbye, Daniel." She clicked the little phone shut as hard as she could. Oh, for the days when a phone could be slammed in a cradle.

She dropped the poor phone on the worktable and leaned forward on her palms, head down, tried to settle. He was right. It had been nine months and she was still struggling. Hearing him voice her fears, in that awful tone, had tears burning her eyes. What if the scumbag was right?

More than that, couldn't he see if he'd really

loved her he'd want her to succeed? Couldn't he see she knew what he really was?

More than all that, though, *what if he was right?*

Beth came in and started toward her in alarm. "Lainey! Are you okay?"

"I'm fine," she said, and wished she meant it. "Daniel just called."

Beth sucked in a breath. "What? Wow, he's got some nerve."

She gave a sharp laugh. "Daniel's got nothing *but* nerve."

Her feelings must have shown on her face because Beth leaned in. "Listen to me. Don't you dare let him get to you. Look at what you've done here. It took a lot of guts to divorce him and buy this place. To keep your parents at arm's length despite their meddling. It hasn't been easy but you're doing it. Don't let them derail you now."

Lainey stared at her friend. "I never—you see it that way?"

Beth leaned over and gave her a one-armed hug. "Of course. And you should, too."

Lainey had never thought of it that way. Oh, she did what needed to be done, but usually well after it should have been done to begin with. Long after she'd been taken for a fool. It didn't strike her as something to be proud of.

The chime of the front door saved her from answering. "I'll get that," she said, and slipped past Beth.

Her friend's words were kind, but Lainey could only hope she was right. There was too much riding on her being able to make this work.

Ben wouldn't admit it to anyone, but he'd been listening for her car.

When he saw her park at the curb he tried to squelch a completely inappropriate spurt of anticipation. He told himself he didn't want this, didn't want her, but every time he saw her it got a little harder to believe it. So he'd rather be anywhere than here, having her help him paint. Just having her in the same house made his skin feel too tight.

Before, he would have asked her out. Seen where it went. But that was—before.

Now he needed to keep his distance—something he wasn't doing very well at.

He heard her come in the front door and turned his attention to finishing taping the bedroom so she could paint. Heard her quick, light steps coming down the hall. He tensed even more as she came in the room.

"Hi." Her voice was slightly tentative, as if she expected to be shot down.

He turned and simply took in the sight of her in old jeans, an oversize sweatshirt, her hair pulled up in a ponytail. She plucked at the sweatshirt uncertainly and he realized he was just standing there, gaping at her like a fool.

He cleared his throat. "Hi. You ready?"

She moved into the room a little farther. So as not to spook her, and to give himself some space, he busied himself popping the top off the paint can.

She came to stand beside him. "I can't wait to see this."

She'd gone to the hardware store on her lunch hour to pick the colors. He'd gone in later to pick them up. Efficient.

She made a little humming noise in her throat. "That's a little pinker than I thought."

"It'll look different once you get it on the wall. It will dry darker. They all do." He set the can off to the side. "You know how to do this?"

He looked up in time to see her shake her head.

He stood up. "You can change a tire, but have never painted a room?"

She looked a little sheepish. "Ah. No. My skills are a bit scattered, I'm afraid."

He didn't want to find that sweet. Or charming. *Damn it.* He turned back to the paint cans and cleared his throat. "Lucky for you, it's easier than changing a tire."

She laughed. "I hope so."

He stirred it and tipped the can to pour into a paint tray. He handed her a paintbrush. "This is pretty simple. You'll do around the trim first. I taped in here already."

He explained the method and showed her how to make small, careful strokes, taking care not to touch her. But she seemed to take equal care not to touch him. She smelled so good it was hard not to give in to temptation.

"When that's done you can do the rest. The roller's pretty simple. Just don't get too much paint on it. You'll be okay in here? I've got some other things to finish up."

Translation: he needed some space. Quickly.

She gave him a small smile and moved the ladder over by the open window. "I'll be fine. I'll call you if I need you."

Dismissed. He walked down the hall toward the kitchen, rubbing his hand over his face. He needed to get this house finished quickly, before the woman in the bedroom back there drove him out of his mind.

When Ben returned to check on Lainey it had only been a half-hour. He'd stayed away as long as he could, which was pitiful. He found her on the ladder by the window, carefully painting under the crown molding. He took a moment to admire the long, lean lines of her legs and the curve of her ass, which was hugged nicely by her soft jeans. Her sweatshirt lifted when she extended her arms up to paint, but not quite enough to give him more than a small but tantalizing glimpse of skin. He tried to shut the feelings down—kissing her had been a mistake because it had unleashed a whole torrent of feelings he didn't want. Couldn't afford. And he was now swamped with them.

This was bad.

She shifted then and he stepped fully into

the room. The last thing he wanted was to get caught staring and make things even more weird. "Lainey—"

She turned quickly on the ladder and upset it enough to lose her balance. With a little cry, she fell awkwardly on her rear on the hard floor.

He crossed the room in about two strides. "Lainey! Are you okay?"

She twisted to sit up, wincing. The floor was hard and he imagined it had been quite a landing. She grabbed her ankle with a sharp hiss.

He knelt beside her, worry clouding his vision. "Honey. Are you okay?" When she shook her head he pulled up her jeans leg to see her ankle starting to swell. "We'd better get that checked out. You might need an X-ray."

Her gaze swung to his and he saw the horror and worry there. She shook her head. "No. No X-rays." She gave a forced little laugh. "I'm just clumsy."

"Your ankle—"

"No."

He sat back. "Lainey, listen—"

"I'm pregnant," she whispered and he drew back to stare at her.

The word rang in his head. *Pregnant.* And he'd been kissing her and wanting her—someone else's woman.

She must have seen the expression change on his face because she grabbed his arm. "The father—he's not in the picture. I'm in this alone. My balance is off. That's why I fell. And X-rays might be bad for the baby."

"What kind of man walks out on his responsibility?" he said, not really expecting an answer, but outraged on her behalf.

She gave a humorless little laugh. "One who misrepresented himself. I'll be fine." She tugged her pant leg back down. "I have to ask—no one but my friend Beth knows this yet... Please—don't say anything to Rose. I'll tell her, but..." She hesitated. "I didn't mean to tell you."

"I understand. I won't. But the father—" For some reason he seemed to be stuck on that fact more than anything.

She cut him off with a slash of her hand. "He knows. He's not on board, so to speak."

A surge of anger welled in Ben. A baby should have a father. And here was a man, apparently alive and well, not willing to take on the responsibility for the little life that he'd created. A responsibility that a good man, like Jason, hadn't been able to keep even though he'd wanted to. "His loss."

Her gaze shot to his and she grimaced slightly. "Damn straight. Can you help me stand?"

"Let me check that ankle first." At her confused expression, he added, "I'm a firefighter and an EMT. I'm not a substitute for a doctor or an X-ray, but I may be able to tell if it's broken."

"Oh." She extended her leg slowly and inched up her jeans.

He removed her shoe carefully but didn't miss her wince. With careful fingers he probed her slim ankle. Her skin was smooth and soft and he was a total heel for his completely unprofessional physical response to touching her.

"I don't feel anything broken," he said. "Let me help you stand."

He got to his feet and took both of her hands in his, trying not to feel the heat her soft touch generated in him. He gave a gentle pull and she hopped up on one foot, overbalanced, and landed on his chest. His arms went around her before he could stop them and he looked down into her beautiful, upturned face. There was confusion and pain and heat and wanting in her blue gaze, and his groin tightened at the press of her breasts against his chest.

He cleared his throat. Kissing her was *not an option. Not an option, not an option,* chanted the loop in his brain, but he wanted so badly to lose himself in it, in her, in this—

Pregnant woman.

He cleared his throat and loosened his hold but didn't let her go fully. "So...um...how's the ankle?" His voice was a little rough.

She rested it on the floor and pulled back a bit, putting a little weight on it. Her wince spoke volumes and he steadied her with his hands on her waist. "Lainey. Please. I know I didn't feel anything broken but some types of breaks I wouldn't necessarily feel. Do you need to go to the hospital?"

She gave a little hopping motion and moved backwards. "No. I'm okay. It's sore, but I can take acetaminophen for it. I want to finish this."

Somehow she hadn't upended the paint when she fell off the ladder, even though she'd dropped the brush on the drop cloth. He took the tray off and poured the paint back in the can so he wouldn't reach for her again. She'd felt far too good in his arms.

But she was pregnant. And even with the father out of the picture he couldn't risk a relationship with her or her baby. He wasn't that kind of guy. Not anymore.

"We'll finish tomorrow. Right now you need to get that ankle up with ice on it. Don't argue," he added when she opened her sexy little mouth to do just that. "And I want you to promise me you'll go in tomorrow if it's worse or not getting better."

She pressed her lips together, then nodded. "Okay. You're right."

"I'll drive you home. You'll need help up to your apartment, right?" He'd get her home, get her settled. It was the least he could do for her, for his grandma's friend. "Tomorrow I'll bring you your car. Leave me your key."

He saw all the arguments cross her face. "I don't want you to go to any trouble—"

"No trouble." He caught her chin, unable to stop the action. The surprise in her eyes licked him like fire. "Lainey. You need a little help. You need to be careful so you don't hurt the baby."

That got her attention and she nodded. "Right. Okay. Thank you."

He swung her into his arms. She let out a little, "Eeep!" and her arms went around his neck.

He gave a little chuckle, surprised by the sound. "Relax. I've got you."

The scary part was how damn good she felt in his arms. How right. How oddly protective he felt of the baby. He hadn't seen the swell of her belly, but her sweatshirt prevented that.

He cut his thoughts off right there. There was nowhere for this to go that could end well. He would be leaving as soon as he had his grandma squared away and his confidence back. He'd only hurt Lainey and he couldn't bring himself to risk it.

CHAPTER SIX

WHAT WAS SHE thinking?

Lainey winced as she buckled her seat belt and Ben walked around the truck to get in. Holy cow. She'd just blurted out her secret to this man, and she hadn't even told his grandma—her friend— yet. Somehow her filter kept shutting off and then her mouth took over.

"I'm not the type who sleeps around," she blurted as soon as he got in the truck. *Ack!* There went the filter again. Maybe it was the pain in her ankle? Yet for some reason it was very important he understand.

He fitted the key in the ignition. His jaw was tense. "I didn't say you were. Things happen."

Yes, they did. She was living proof that *things* tended to happen to some people more than others. She stared out the window, not wanting to see him even in profile, lit by the dash lights. It wasn't his fault he kept showing up when she was falling apart, though it had happened with alarming frequency since she'd met him.

The drive home was tense but Lainey had no desire to talk. Her ankle throbbed and she tried to focus on that rather than the fact she'd told Ben about the baby. Told an almost perfect stranger who'd kissed her, for God's sake. There was a kind of intimacy that they were both pretty good at ignoring. And she'd just added to it by blurting out that she was pregnant. A little panic raised its head. It had been far, far easier to tell him than it should have been. What was it about him that made her spill her secrets? Was it because he was so different from her ex-husband? She frowned. Even that didn't fully make sense, since she barely knew him. But something about him spoke to her, soothed her. Almost as if she recognized him somehow, on a deeper level.

She gave herself a mental shake. Wow. That really didn't make sense. Maybe she'd somehow managed to hit her head when she fell. Or the pain in her ankle was making her a little crazy.

Ben pulled in front of the shop and she reached down to unbuckle the seat belt. "Well. Thanks for the ride," she said brightly. "Sorry to put you out."

He caught her hand. In the dim glow of the streetlights, he looked as surprised as she was at the contact. "You could never put me out. Stay there. Please. Let me help you down."

"I can—"

"Of course you can," he interrupted. "But you don't want to risk a fall that might hurt the baby or further damage the ankle. And you might need some help navigating those stairs."

Darn it. He was right. "Okay."

He gave her a small smile before he slipped out of the truck. "It's okay to need help, Lainey."

She watched him walk in front of the truck through the wash of the headlights and couldn't help but think he wasn't totally correct. Needing help didn't make her weak, but it left her open to people like her parents and their manipulations. It was safer to rely on herself than sort through the motivations of others.

He opened the door and reached for her. It was a little awkward to slide out into his arms, and she was surprised when he didn't put her down, instead settled her into his arms. She didn't want to admit how good the hardness of his chest felt against her side, how incredibly good he smelled.

"This is easier if you relax a little," he said close to her ear.

She looked up to see humor spark in his eyes. The humor died, though, when his gaze fell to her mouth and his arms tightened perceptibly around her.

She caught her breath at the dark heat she saw there and an answering one rose in her. It wouldn't take much, just a slight shift...

A car drove by and the spell was snapped. He cleared his throat and started for the door.

Her face burned. Good Lord, what *was* this?

She forced herself to relax into his solid chest. Weird moments aside, it felt good to lean on someone. Just for a minute. His heart beat faster against her ribs. Its rhythm matched that of her own and she wondered if it was from the moment they'd shared or the exertion of carrying her. The coolness of the evening did nothing to counteract the warmth he generated in her.

He got her upstairs and she unlocked her door.

"Sit," he said as he steered her gently toward the couch, and she sank down gratefully.

He put a pillow under the ankle. She couldn't help but notice how he sucked all the air out of the room and made her small space seem even tinier.

"I'll get you ice and some acetaminophen. Where do you keep it?"

"Bathroom, in the medicine cabinet," she said, adjusting the pillow. Not because it needed it but because then she didn't have to look at him and see—what? Or maybe, more accurately, he wouldn't see what kind of effect he had on her.

"All right." He went in the kitchen. "Hey, kitty," she heard him say, and her heart tilted just a bit. Then, in a louder voice, "Where are the glasses? And do I need to feed the cat? She's looking at me like she expects something."

She swallowed a laugh. "She does. There's a can of food in the fridge. You can put the rest of it in her dish. And glasses are in the cupboard to the right of the sink."

She listened to the sounds in the kitchen, the low murmur of his voice as he talked to the cat, the opening and closing of the cupboard, the rattling of ice. She rested her head on the back of the couch and shut her eyes. No one had ever taken care of her before. Such a little thing—ice for her ankle, feeding the cat, water for the pills. Not earth-shattering. Yet it was somehow.

He appeared with the items and placed ice, wrapped in a towel, over her ankle. "That okay?"

The gentleness of the action nearly undid her. She swallowed hard. "Yes. Thanks."

"Here's the water. Hold on while I get the pills."

He headed down the hall, looking first to the left—her bedroom—then to the right—her bathroom. Where she'd thrown bras she'd hand-washed over the shower rod. She shut her eyes in mortification. There was a brief pause as he entered the bathroom—no doubt he'd gotten an eyeful—then the rattling of the pill bottle. When he came back down the hall he didn't actually make eye contact. Then again, neither did she.

"Here you go." He plopped the pills in her palm. Was it just her, or were his fingers slightly unsteady? "Can I call anyone for you?"

She almost laughed. "No. I'm all set, thanks."

He cleared his throat. "All right, then. I'll bring you your car tomorrow. If you need anything, call me. Where's your phone?"

She tugged her purse over and pulled the phone out. He took it from her and added his number.

"Now you have no excuse. I'm serious. Especially if you need help with those stairs in the morning." He handed the phone back and this time their fingers lingered for a heartbeat.

Breathless, she tried to smile. "I will. Um… thank you. For everything."

He stepped back. "No problem."

When the door shut behind him she flopped back on the cushions and pressed both hands over her eyes, unsure if she should laugh or scream.

She was in way deeper trouble than she'd thought.

Ben stared at the game on the TV above the bar. He couldn't have told anyone who was playing, much less the score, and he was only vaguely aware it was a hockey game. All he could see was Lainey's perfect mouth forming the words *"I'm pregnant"*.

They still packed a punch. It wasn't even his kid, and he'd never meet the baby—no doubt he'd be long gone by the time Lainey gave birth. In fact, it was most likely he'd never talk to her again, unless they ran into each other though Rose somehow. So why the hell did it matter?

He shifted on the stool. Lainey was dangerous. The kind of dangerous that made him want what he couldn't have. It wasn't fair to Jason—or Callie, for that matter. What right did he have even to think about pursuing a woman—Lainey—when Callie's husband was gone?

He took a swallow of the beer he couldn't even taste. He was pretty sure the bitterness in his mouth came from his own feelings rather than the drink in his hand.

Pregnant.

He'd felt a stab of jealousy straight to his soul when she'd looked at him with those big blue eyes and whispered those words. No use passing it off as anything but that.

What could he offer her? He didn't even know if he could do his job anymore. That anxiety was ever-present, hovering in the back of his mind. Shading everything he did. It mixed with guilt into a potent brew of shame and sorrow.

So, no, he wasn't in any shape to pursue her. Therefore, being jealous was a complete waste of time and energy. Still, he'd felt a roaring protectiveness when she'd fallen. And far more than that when he'd walked in her bathroom and seen those lacy, sexy bras lined up on the shower rod.

God help him. He was getting in way over his head and all he'd done was help her. But something about her drew him in and he couldn't seem to walk away. All those feelings he'd walled off…? Yeah. He was in danger of drowning in them if he didn't get them under control fast.

It didn't matter. He set aside his half-empty beer, since he couldn't even taste it, and signaled for his bill. He wasn't getting anywhere having a pity party and it was a waste of time anyway. Might as well go home, where there were at least projects he could do to stay busy.

He entered the house quietly, but his sharp-eyed grandma was in the living room, knitting. He couldn't tell what it was but her hands flew and the needles clicked together sharply. She looked up when he came in.

"So. How was it?"

Ben sat down opposite her, since it seemed rude to stand and talk when she was all settled in. He outlined the progress he'd made on the house, then hesitated.

Rose arched a brow. "What?"

He debated how much he could say and keep Lainey's secret safe. "She twisted her ankle," he said finally. "Stepped wrong off the ladder."

Rose's hands stopped moving. "Is she okay?"

"I checked it out," he said. "She was adamant about not going to the hospital."

"She needs an X-ray," Rose muttered and Ben sighed.

"I suggested it but she shot me down." True enough.

Rose sighed and her needles started moving again. "I bet."

"I offered to call her mother, but she said no." He wasn't fishing, exactly, but he was curious as to why Lainey seemed to think she was on her own when she had family nearby.

Rose snorted. "That woman doesn't have a maternal bone in her body. And that ex of hers—" She pressed her lips together tightly. "Well. Anyway. I'd better call her—make sure she's okay. I wish you'd brought her back here."

Ben was pretty sure Lainey didn't want Rose to figure out about the pregnancy. As Rose dialed Lainey's number he took a good look at the knitting project on her lap. The soft colors and small size looked an awful lot like a baby blanket. But he wasn't going to ask any questions.

They'd each keep Lainey's secret.

He hung around, fixing himself something to eat he really didn't want in the kitchen, but he wasn't going to admit that. When he went back in the living room Rose was hanging up and frowning.

That protective instinct reared back up and he forced himself to keep his voice level. "Is she okay?"

Rose's gaze flicked to his. "She's hurting."

Ben started to stand. "I can go—"

Rose shook her head. "She won't come. Thinks she has to be strong." She gave him a pointed look. "Like someone else I know."

He opted not to touch that comment. "I've got to get her car to her tomorrow."

"That's good. Then you can see if she's okay in person. She's likely to not admit it over the phone."

She had a point.

He cleared his throat. "Sounds good. You need anything before I go take a shower?"

Rose shook her head, her hands flying once

more over the blanket. "Thank God for DVR. Got one more show to watch. I'm all set, thanks."

He chuckled and walked toward the stairs. She said his name softly. When he turned, she looked at him, her faded blue gaze serious.

"She needs someone like you."

Ben froze as the words pinged around in his heart. "No. No, I'm not what she needs."

"Ben." Her voice was sharp. "You are exactly what she needs. Don't sell yourself short."

He had nothing to say to that. As he went up the stairs his heart was heavy. He wasn't what Lainey needed. He was too damaged to be enough for anyone.

Still. He regretted not being able to have the chance.

Where there's smoke, there's fire.

Ben could see the black plume of smoke the next morning from the front porch of his grandma's house, where he'd been working on the ramp. It was coming from the other side of town. *Lainey's side.*

That thought bumped him into action. He'd go check on her, make sure—just make sure. Since he had to take her car back anyway, this gave him the excuse. And she wouldn't be moving real fast after that fall, so no one would think twice if he checked on her.

"I'm going to take Lainey's car back," he told his grandma, who was in the kitchen with her Sudoku book. "You need anything while I'm out?"

She tipped her glasses down her nose. "Everything okay?"

He hesitated. "There's a fire."

She gave a small nod. "We've got good people here, Ben. Maybe you should be one of them?"

He opened his mouth, then shut it again. He shook his head, grabbed his jacket from by the back door and hurried to his truck.

It only took a few minutes to drive to the other house. From this angle it was hard to tell precisely where the fire was, but he could smell the smoke. He flexed his hands on the wheel as he turned onto the street and pulled into the rental house's driveway. He started Lainey's car and headed for downtown.

He whipped the car into a spot down the block from Lainey's shop and jogged across the street toward the smoke. He needed to see, to know if he could handle it. Now he could see ash floating in the air, and he heard the wail of sirens. Tension built in his shoulders and he rolled them in an effort to release it.

He took a deep breath of the smoky air and coughed as he turned down a side street to see a fully engulfed building. He stayed well back from the cordoned-off area. Fire didn't fascinate him the way it did other people. It was an enemy, a force, a beast to be tamed and conquered. Seeing it lick gleefully at the building gave him no thrill.

He watched the firefighters doing their job—*his* job—and swallowed hard. This was what he was born to do, but he wasn't sure he could ever go back. God, but he missed it. He missed it like he'd miss his arm if he'd lost it. Missed the adrenaline, the teamwork. The battle. It could be grim work—messy, and damn hard—but, hell, there wasn't anything else he'd rather do.

When the roof caved in with a shower of sparks and the flames leapt higher he shut his eyes as nausea rolled over him. For a second he couldn't breathe. Finally he turned and walked away, disappointment lodging in his gut like a rock.

He'd wondered—now he knew. He wasn't ready. Would he ever be?

He stopped in front of The Lily Pad, its bright windows and festive decor drawing him like a beacon through the cool, smoky air. He didn't want to examine his relief at finding her shop okay or his anger at himself for his reaction to the fire. Or the real reason the shop pulled him: the woman inside.

Every step closer tangled everything tighter inside him.

He pushed it all away and walked through the door.

Lainey looked up and gave him a small, startled smile. He didn't miss the flash of pleasure that crossed her beautiful face.

"Ben."

He tamped down his own reaction and pulled her key out of his pocket. "Thought I'd stop by and give you this." He moved forward and shook his head when she started to get up. "No, sit. How's the ankle?"

"Better today." She held out her hand and he pressed the key into her palm. Her skin was warm under his cool fingers. Her eyes widened slightly at the contact and he wondered if she felt it, too. The heat, the spark.

Sparks.

"Did you see the fire?" She shook her head as she slipped the key into her pocket. "Of course you must have. I can smell the smoke on your jacket. You said you're a firefighter, right?"

He cleared his throat, suddenly having trouble breathing. "Yeah. I did. I was." *Was.* His voice stuck a little on the word. Was he or wasn't he? Could he ever go back? What if he couldn't?

"Ben?" The concern in her voice made him wince. "Are you okay? You looked a little lost there for a moment."

Lost. That was a good word for him. "I'm fine. Sorry."

She studied him, and for a second he thought she'd ask him more questions. But her phone rang. She glanced at it, then at him.

"I'll get out of here." So he wouldn't touch her, he put his hands in his pockets. "Your car's down about half a block."

"Thank you," she murmured as the phone rang. "I appreciate it."

He didn't hang around as she answered the

phone, but he did pause at the door and look back. Her eyes were on him and she blushed just a little as her gaze caught his. He swallowed hard and walked out into the smoky fall air.

Lainey let out a shuddering breath as she hung up the phone from an order. She'd managed to get all the information, but it had been hard, seeing Ben through the windows as he'd walked, slightly hunched against the wind, past the windows of her shop. She'd hoped—foolishly—he'd look back at her one more time. *Silly.*

She entered the last of the order information into the computer and stretched. While her ankle needed to be propped up, the position was uncomfortable for her back.

Beth breezed back in, to-go bag from the café in hand. She shook her head as she placed it on the counter. "Was that Ben I saw walking by? Was he here?"

Lainey took the offered sandwich and set it carefully on a napkin. "Just for a minute. He brought my car up here."

Beth waggled her eyebrows. "Is that all?"

Lainey sighed. His face—so closed up today,

after how sweet he'd been last night. He'd shut down even farther when, in her apparently misguided quest to make conversation, she'd asked him about being a firefighter. Clearly a sore spot. "Yeah. That's all."

Beth clucked her tongue. "Too bad. He's hot. And the two of you would be so cute together."

She thought of how easily she'd fit in his arms last night, and the heat in his eyes, and a little shiver passed through her. "That's silly."

Beth shrugged and snagged a French fry. "Maybe. Maybe not. But you have to start somewhere, Laine."

She stared at her sandwich. No, she didn't. Not really. And Ben wasn't interested in her. Well, actually, that wasn't true. He was clearly interested in her. But he wasn't willing or able to take it anywhere.

And neither was she.

CHAPTER SEVEN

THE DOOR CHIMED and Lainey walked carefully out of the back room, not wanting to admit the little skip in her pulse was the hope it was Ben coming back, no matter how unlikely that was. She'd decided to ask him to her mother's gala, and didn't want to lose her nerve.

It was a complete surprise to see her brother. "Kevin?"

"Hey, little sis," Kevin greeted her with a smile. "What's going on? Mom said you're moving."

Lainey looked at her brother, still in his scrubs. He looked tired, and there were definite lines around his blue eyes, but his smile was warm.

She gestured to him. "Come on back. You stopped in to ask me that?"

"Well, I was on my way to Mel's Café for lunch and thought I'd stop in." When Lainey opened her mouth, he held up his hands. "No, I'm not here to convince you of anything. I'm just asking."

Lainey moved to the worktable and pulled out a length of pumpkin-colored ribbon she was using for a silk centerpiece. Kevin had rarely, if ever, been on the receiving end of their parents' ire. He was a surgeon, lived in an appropriate condo, and drove a nice car. No wife yet, but that wasn't held against him. "Did they tell you what happened?"

Kevin leaned on the table. Now his expression was concerned. "No."

She took a deep breath. "They bought this building."

Kevin cocked his head. "Doesn't it help you out?"

She stabbed a floral pin in with a little more force than necessary. "Kevin. They didn't ask me. They showed me the deed and said I had to move back home."

Kevin swore softly under his breath. "I'm sorry, Laine. Did they say why?"

"Of course. I'm not doing well here. Yet. It's been a struggle. And I guess they don't think that reflects well on them." She didn't mention Daniel. No point in muddying the waters.

"Are you?"

"Am I what?"

"Moving back home?"

She gave a sharp little bark of laughter. "God, no. I found a nice little house a friend of mine owns. I'm moving there—this weekend, in fact."

He chucked her under the chin, a gentle and brotherly gesture. "Good for you. I'm glad you stood up to them."

Emotion flooded her. She'd never really expected him to watch her back. "Thank you."

He stepped back. "Do you need help? I'm on call this weekend, but I can come over if I'm around."

She hesitated. Why not? Beth and her husband were helping, but she could use the extra pair of hands. "Sure. That'd be great."

"All right." He turned to go. "I'll be here at nine unless otherwise noted. That okay?"

"See you then," she said, and watched as he disappeared through the workroom door. Strange to have him in her corner. Maybe she'd walled herself off from her brother with her own feelings of inadequacy and inferiority. If so, shame on her. It seemed Kevin might actually be an ally.

God knew she could use one.

* * *

That evening, Ben looked up from the whine of the saw to see Lainey standing there, her eyes hooded in the dim light of the rental house's garage, her hands twisted into knots in front of her. He hit the switch on the saw and silenced it.

"Hey."

She swallowed hard. "Hey."

He came toward her and she tipped her head back to look at him. He saw anxiety swimming in her eyes and he closed his hand into a fist to keep from stroking her face.

"Let's go outside—out of the dust." He took her elbow and lightly steered her toward the porch.

"What are you doing in there?"

"Repairing one of the cabinet doors. Do you need some help with the painting?"

She shook her head and her hair bounced lightly on her shoulders. He caught a hint of a lightly fruity shampoo. "Actually, I need you."

The words stopped him cold, even as a spear of heat shot through his belly. It would be no hardship to have her need him, but of course she hadn't meant it that way. He cleared his throat. "For what?"

She paced across the front lawn, kicking at the leaves. "I feel so stupid. I wouldn't ask you if I wasn't desperate."

Ben was pretty sure that was his ego, flying away in shreds. "Desperate?"

"Oh!" She spun back around and her cheeks were bright pink—a huge improvement over the paleness they'd held a few minutes ago. "I didn't mean— I just meant—"

"It's fine," he interrupted. "What do you need?"

She stared at the sky for a minute and he wondered if she was looking for a lightning bolt.

"A date."

He couldn't have heard her right. A date? He didn't date—even casually. If he did date, it definitely wouldn't be a woman who was in danger of making him feel things again. He opened his mouth to tell her so but she rushed on.

"My mother hosts this fundraiser gala thing at the hospital every year. I need to go, and I don't have a date. I was hoping maybe you'd come with me."

"When is it?" God, was he actually considering it? He'd meant to say *no way*.

"Next Thursday." When he said nothing she

turned even pinker and turned to walk away. "You know…this was a bad idea. I'm sorry. I'll just go alone."

He crossed to her in two steps. "Black tie?" Hell, he hated black tie.

She swallowed. "Yes."

"I'll go." Holy hell, what was he thinking?

"It's okay—" she started, then stopped as his words sank in. Her eyes widened. "You will?"

He nodded.

"Oh, thank you," she breathed, and flung her arms around him for a brief, tight hug. "Thank you."

He couldn't resist teasing a little. "Only because you're desperate." Hell. He was getting soft. He couldn't possibly be letting her get to him. Right?

She pulled away, but he looped his arms around her back and held her against him, wanting to feel her for a moment. Her gaze caught his and the world fell away for a minute. Heat wove around them, lazy and slow, and his gaze dropped to her mouth. The memory of that kiss in the park hung between them—her warm, sweet mouth and hungry response. He wanted it. Especially now, with her pink cheeks and slightly parted lips tempting him to claim them.

She made a little sound in her throat and he let her go, setting her away from him. Her gaze refocused, then bounced away, landing anywhere but on him.

"So…ah…I'll get going," she said, edging toward her car. "I'll see you later."

"Yeah." He marshaled his thoughts away from kissing her. It took way more effort than he wanted to admit. "What time for the gala?"

"It starts at seven—so say, six-thirty?"

"All right," he said, and she hurried to her car and hopped in. As he watched her drive down the road he wondered where the hell he'd find a tux by next Thursday night.

He strode back to the garage. Then he fished his cell out of his pocket. First things first. He wouldn't let Lainey down.

It seemed the harder Ben tried to keep his distance, the more he was drawn to Lainey.

It wasn't good.

He locked the little house up behind him. Lainey had gone home after painting. They'd managed to avoid any more awkward moments like they'd had outside. It seemed the best thing he could do was bump up his timetable. He'd finished the ramp for his grandma just today, and he was nearly done with this rental house. So there weren't any real reasons to stick around once he'd gotten his grandma squared away. It would be best to get away from Lainey before he got any more involved with her.

Which was why it had floored him when he said he'd go with her to that party. That wasn't the way to keep his distance.

He scrubbed a hand over his face with a sigh. While he wasn't ready to go back to firefighting yet, there was really no reason not to go back to Grand Rapids.

Well, there was Callie and her broken family. He blew out a breath. He couldn't go back yet. He wasn't ready. He couldn't even return Callie's phone calls. Eventually she'd quit trying. One more thing to add to the morass of guilt.

He'd finish up the house, go to the gala, and that would be the end of the contact he had with Lainey. He'd make excuses and leave when she came to visit. It would be easier on both of them. She wanted to see his grandma, anyway, not him.

He cleaned up his mess and drove back to his grandma's house. As he got out of his truck a car turned in the driveway behind him. Grandma—coming home from her knitting group, he thought. She had a very full social calendar, which amused him no end. And pleased him, too.

He walked up to the car and opened her door. She beamed up at him. "Hello, Ben."

"Hi, Grandma."

He went around back when the driver popped the trunk and pulled the wheelchair out. Then he held it steady as his grandma moved from the car to the chair. As much as he hated to see her like this, he had to admit she handled it with grace and humor.

"Thank you," she said, and waved at her friend. Ben helped her wheel up the ramp into the house.

"This ramp is wonderful," she said as they came in the door. "I can't tell you how much easier it is going to make my life. I appreciate it so much."

Ben shut the door behind them, uncomfortable with her gratitude. He didn't deserve it. He'd been gone for too long, and she'd needed him. Lainey had been right about that when they'd first met. "I'm glad," was all he said.

She wheeled around to face him, a frown on her face as she put her knitting bag on the floor by her favorite chair. "It was an honest compliment," she said quietly. "It's okay to accept it."

He shoved his hands in his pockets. "I know. I just feel like I should have been here long before now."

She sighed. "I could have let you know, Ben. I was very clear that I didn't want to worry you. This isn't all on you. As you can see, I've got a very solid support system. I've been managing. And I am very grateful you took this time to help me out. That is all I meant."

He knew that, but it was hard to let go of the self-recrimination. He'd held on to it like a shield for the past week or so, using it to keep his distance.

"So," she said. "Is the house ready for Lainey?"

Grateful for the topic-change, he said, "Pretty much. I'm still working on some minor repairs. But, yes, it's otherwise ready."

She gave a little nod. "Excellent. She's moving this weekend, then?"

"Far as I know." He opted not to mention yet that she'd asked him to the gala. That might put ideas in Grandma's head he didn't want her to have. She liked Lainey, and he didn't want to get her hopes up.

Or your own?

Choosing to ignore that particular thought, he shoved his hands in his pockets. "It'll be all ready for her. You can call her and firm up the date and time."

Rose cocked her head. "You've got a truck," she said thoughtfully. "It might go faster if you offered to help."

Ben swallowed hard. Of course it would. Lainey's car wasn't nearly big enough to haul furniture. And he wasn't going to *not* help her because he was so damn terrified of her. "When you call her, tell her I offered."

She didn't push. "I will. Thank you, Ben."

"Sure," he said, not adding, *I'd do it for anyone.* Because he was afraid that wasn't true.

Lainey's cell buzzed. The number was the same area code as she'd dialed for Jon. Her stomach instantly fell. Beth had left for deliveries so she was alone. She took a deep breath and answered.

"Hello?"

"Lainey. It's Jon." His voice was crisp. "Wanted to let you know we've drawn up the paperwork to begin the process for me to terminate my rights. It's been overnighted to you."

Lainey froze for a moment. This was what she wanted, but somehow saying *thank you* seemed both wrong and inadequate. "I—okay. I'll look out for it."

There was the slightest of pauses, then he cleared his throat. "Best of luck to you, Lainey."

She turned and stared out the window at the cars passing by. "You too. You're going to need it far more than I will."

He barked a laugh, even though she hadn't been trying to be funny. "Don't I know it? From here on out if you have any questions refer them to my lawyer."

"I can't imagine I'd have any need," she said. "But okay."

She clicked the phone shut in her hand. Slowly the import of the conversation began to sink in. She was well and truly a single mother now. Relief mixed with sorrow that it had gone this way. That she'd given her baby a man like Jon for a father. A man who would sign his rights away rather than tell his wife. Instead of a man like Ben.

She sighed and slipped the phone in her pocket. Ben would leave, too. He'd been clear that he was only here for a short time, and even more telling, that his attraction to her was reluctant at best. Something he couldn't help rather than something he actually wanted.

She'd do well to keep that in mind.

"Geez, sis, what do you have in these boxes?"

Kevin's grumbled question on Saturday morning made Lainey smile.

"Rocks—just for you," she teased, and saw Kevin frown out the window. "What?"

"You expecting someone? Big truck. Tall guy. Wait—is that Ben Lawless?"

Lainey's heart skipped. "Yes." It was a good thing he could help, since Beth and her husband hadn't been able to come after all.

"Our job just got easier. He's got a lot of room

in that truckbed. Let's get these boxes out of the way so we can move the furniture."

Ben came up the stairs and Lainey tried very hard not to flush or otherwise react in case her brother picked up on anything. As it was, she'd taken care to dress in clothes that hid her slightly rounded midsection, without being obvious about it. She couldn't take the chance that Kevin's doctor eye would spot what she wasn't ready for him to see.

Ben's greeting was a nod, before he turned his attention to Kevin and they launched into a moving strategy discussion. Feeling oddly left out, Lainey slipped into her bedroom, where she'd left a couple boxes of fragile items she didn't want mixed in with the rest of her things.

It only took a few trips. It was a little depressing that her life had been reduced to a couple of car and truckloads, including the furniture. Now it was all in her new house, somewhat willy-nilly, though the guys *had* asked her where she wanted things. Kevin had left after the last trip, and Ben was coming back with a few miscellaneous items.

Lainey went in the kitchen. If she started in

there she would be able to at least eat a bowl of cereal or soup. When the front door opened her pulse kicked up. She'd managed to keep Kevin between them. Not too hard, considering they were the ones doing the heavy lifting. But now she and Ben were alone.

She ripped open the box closest to her and found her dishes. She heard Ben's steps in the hall and rose from the floor to greet him. He leaned on the wall and surveyed the mess.

"You've got your work cut out for you," he observed, and she took the opportunity to turn and examine the chaos.

"Yep. It will take me a couple days, but I'll get it all done." Not sure what to do now, she hesitated, then stuck out her hand. "Thank you. I appreciate your help."

He paused just a heartbeat before he took her hand in response. His palm, warm and rough, sent shivers up her arm. What would it feel like on her skin?

She released his hand and stepped back, willing the thoughts away. He shoved his hands in his pockets. She didn't know how to make the awkwardness stop—wasn't even sure it was the best thing to do.

He cleared his throat. "Grandma's invited you to lunch at Mel's Café. She'll be there—" he glanced at his watch "—in about fifteen minutes."

"Oh. That's wonderful, but I think I need to get cracking on this." Practically on cue, her stomach growled loudly and he arched a brow.

"What are you going to eat? One of these boxes?"

Humor glimmered in his eyes and it took her breath away because she knew how rare it was to see it.

"I—well, yeah. Maybe with peanut butter?" She grinned at him and was rewarded with a small smile. Which for him was an ear-to-ear grin.

"We can do better than that," he said dryly. "Come on. I'll drive you."

Unable to think of a suitable excuse—and really she didn't want one, she was hungry—she grabbed her purse and followed him out the door, which she locked with her new key. He opened the passenger door and she climbed in.

"How is Rose getting there?" she asked when he got in the other side.

"A friend took her to get her hair and nails done this morning. She'll drop Grandma off."

Lainey frowned. "How will she get home? This truck is awful high." His expression was shuttered and she realized he'd taken it as a criticism. "I didn't mean that as anything other than a statement of fact," she added stiffly.

He didn't touch her comment. "She's got something else going on after lunch."

"Oh." Lainey stared out the window, mentally kicking herself for her thoughtlessness. It seemed every step they took forward was quickly followed by three back. Such an awkward dance they were doing—trying to be ultra-polite while pretending there was nothing between them.

It was exhausting.

She unbuckled when he'd parked at the café, just down from her shop and her now-former apartment. Once they entered the café she saw Rose at a table by the window. The older woman waved and Lainey waved back. She slid into the seat across from Rose and was surprised when Ben sat next to her. Until she realized Rose had taken over the second seat with her coat and purse. In spite of herself, she wondered if it had been intentional. Was Rose matchmaking? She wouldn't put it past her friend.

"Love your hair," Lainey said, admiring the soft curls, and Rose patted it.

"She did a good job, didn't she? Makes me look good."

Lainey laughed and caught Rose's hand. "What color is this?" It was a deep pink, a perfect shade for her skin and her silver hair. It occurred to her *she* hadn't had a manicure since she'd divorced Daniel. Not that it mattered, but was one more sign of how much her life had changed.

"I can't remember exactly. It had peony in the name."

"Did you order?" Lainey asked, and Rose shook her head.

"Not yet. But I know what I'm getting."

The waitress came over and Rose ordered a club sandwich, Lainey a turkey sandwich, and Ben something big with roast beef.

Rose sat back. "So. Did you get it all moved?"

She glanced at Ben. "Yes. Ben and Kevin made

it look easy. I guess it helped I didn't have that much stuff."

Ben stretched his legs out in front of him and bumped her thigh in the process. She sucked in a breath.

"Sure seemed like a lot for one woman and a cat."

His low, teasing tone gave her goosebumps. She smacked him lightly on the arm, trying desperately not to respond to him. *Rose is here.* The mental reminder didn't work.

"Not that much," she said with a laugh, and saw Rose watching them with an expression that could only be described as thoughtful. Lainey sighed inwardly. The undercurrents between them were on full display.

So much for not feeding the matchmaking fire.

CHAPTER EIGHT

LAINEY'S WEEKEND PASSED in a flurry of unpacking. While the end result was a little sparse, she wasn't worried. One thing she'd always loved was finding treasures at places like thrift shops and garage sales. One more thing her mother had never understood. So she'd keep an eye out for what she might need.

Well, after baby needs, of course. That was her next project. Setting up the nursery.

In fact she stood in the room in question right now. Nothing was in here yet. She'd left it empty on purpose. She needed a crib, a changing table… Maybe she could find a dresser that could do double duty. A rocker for the corner. A bookcase for toys and such. She left the room, a smile on her face, and walked back though the house. Being here felt right. Panda sat in a spot of sunlight on the kitchen floor. While the cat hadn't been pleased about the car ride, she'd settled in once she'd found her food and water bowls, as well as her litter box. Lainey was hopeful come spring she could let the cat out into the fenced-in backyard.

She padded into her bedroom to get dressed. And frowned when her low-rise jeans didn't snap. Yesterday they'd fit—albeit a bit snug. Today, no dice. That meant two things.

One: full-time maternity clothes.

Two: telling her family.

Lainey shut her eyes. The moment of truth was here. Her father was out of town, so she'd have to tell her mother alone. She'd do it after work, when she returned the apartment keys.

She left the house with a little fizzle of joy as she used her new key to lock it up behind her, and drove to the shop. As was her habit now, she checked the cooler temperature first thing. It was running a tick above where she wanted it, but it had been holding fairly steady.

Beth walked in a few minutes later. "Hey, Laine. How was the move?"

"Pretty smooth," she answered.

"Was it just you and Kevin? Aw, Laine. I'm so sorry we couldn't be there. We should have—"

"You should have gone to visit your father-in-law, just like you did. It all worked out. Ben helped, too," Lainey said quickly. "I think Rose asked him to."

A small smile tugged at the corners of Beth's mouth. "Really?" she said, drawing out the word. "How was that?"

Lainey rolled her eyes and stomped over to open the cash register, pretending not to catch her friend's meaning. "A lot of work—what else?"

Beth's low laugh followed her across the room. "Mmm-hmm. Do you think Kevin noticed anything? Lainey, it's pretty obvious there's chemistry with you guys."

Oh, she hoped not. "I don't think so. He's a guy, so he can be pretty oblivious. Plus, I really didn't see Ben that much. They just loaded and unloaded. They were together more than we were." Then she realized what she'd just admitted. "Oh—"

Beth wrapped an arm around Lainey's shoulders and squeezed. "Now all you have to do is stop fighting it. Let yourself just give in."

She stepped away, her point clearly made, and Lainey busied herself with the cash drawer. It wasn't as easy as *just giving in.* There was too much at stake to *just give in.* Why couldn't Beth see that? She wasn't sure she could give in if she wanted to. She was aware of how quickly things could go wrong. Once you'd had your wings clipped, it made it awful hard to get off the ground.

And she was scared to try and fly again.

Lainey turned down her parents' street and her stomach fluttered. Silly, really, since she was an adult. But those old habits of wanting to be a good daughter were hard to break. She'd decided to go in quick, say her piece, and get out. She'd send for the housekeeper if her mother passed out.

The thought made her giggle just a little hysterically. The unflappable Jacqui—completely flapped.

Her mother's car was parked by the garage—a sure sign she'd be heading back out later. Lainey parked in the circle and took a second to brace herself. While it was time, it would be nice if she had someone to back her up, and she almost wished she'd asked Kevin to come along. He'd know how to manage their mother.

She rang the bell and waited. Jacqui answered after a minute, brow arched high. "Lainey. This is a nice surprise. What brings you here?"

She stepped aside and Lainey entered the foyer.

"I need to talk to you for a minute." Her voice was calm, not betraying her nerves. Good.

"Of course. I've got a meeting in a half-hour. Will this take long?"

"I don't think so," Lainey said.

She followed her mother's trim form into the living room and took a deep breath. Once again she tried to imagine a baby on the floor, or pulling itself up on the velvet-covered furniture. She couldn't picture it. Was that because she was afraid her parents wouldn't want her and the baby in their lives? Wasn't that part of what had made her so reluctant to tell them?

It didn't matter now. She took a deep breath. "I have something important to tell you."

"I see." Jacqui crossed to the mini-wet bar. "Well, then. Something to drink? Will you be joining me for dinner?"

Not likely. "No, Mother."

Jacqui turned, a can of ginger ale in her hand, an expectant look on her face. "Well, then, what do you need to tell me, dear?"

There was no point in beating around the bush. "I'm pregnant."

Jacqui gasped, and the color leached from her face as the pop can slid from her hand and landed on the carpet with a fizzy hiss. The golden liquid splashed all over her legs and feet. Frozen for a heartbeat, Lainey leapt up and grabbed a handful of paper towels from the wet bar, almost grateful for the distraction.

"Are you sure?" Jacqui's voice was faint.

Lainey didn't look up from blotting at the mess. She wasn't sure she could look at her mother just yet. "Positive. I'm a little more than two months along." Her hands shook as she dropped the first mass of sopping towels in the garbage under the bar.

Jacqui let out a long exhale. "Good God."

That about sums it up.

"Are you getting married? Who's the father?"

Lainey winced. "No. And the father is no one you know." True enough. Jon wouldn't have been on her parents' radar.

"Ben Lawless?" Her mother nearly spat Ben's name.

Lainey bobbled the paper towel roll. What did her mother have against Ben? "No. Of course not. He'd *want* to be involved in the baby's life." The truth of those words batted against her heart.

"And the father doesn't?"

Lainey couldn't speak over the wave of shame that rose in her. She pressed her lips together instead and shook her head.

Jacqui sighed and stepped out of her sticky heels. "Oh, Lainey. You need to get married, pronto. I wonder if Daniel would be willing to marry you with you carrying someone else's baby? Lainey, *damn it.* I think you just ruined any chance you had with that man!"

Lainey sat back on her heels, temper snapping at her throat. "I already told you I don't care, Mother. I'm not getting married. I will be a single parent. I don't give a damn what Daniel thinks. I'm sure he has kids somewhere. He did enough sowing of the seed, as they say."

Jacqui gasped. "Lainey!"

"Well, he did. If it wore heels, he chased it. He almost never slept with *me*, thank God—who

knows what I could have come down with?—
but he did with other women. At the end he was
bringing them into our home, did you know
that?" The humiliation burned though her all over
again. "I'd be gone, or maybe not. The basement
was his little playboy cave. He could have cared
less about me—about our marriage. He married
me for you and Dad—for your money, for where
your name could take him. So when I grew a
spine and divorced him it really threw him. He's
not back here for *me*, Mother. He wants to get
back in your lives."

Jacqui stared at her, jaw dropped. "Lainey—"
she said finally, then lapsed into silence.

"But you knew, didn't you?" Lainey said softly.
"Some of it, anyway. And it was okay, because
he had the right connections, the right amount
of money. You were willing to look the other
way, like you've done with Dad." The truth arced
through her, sharp and hot.

Jacqui stood very still. "Be very careful, young
lady. You're on dangerous ground now."

Lainey couldn't stop. It was too important.
"He's always been very discreet—unlike Dan-

iel. I'd have thought you'd want better for me than you had. I know I do."

The truth hurt. She loved her father, but she knew his weaknesses. Daniel was just like him, only without the intelligence or compassion. She also knew her father loved her mother, despite his failings. And that was between them. Not her business.

She stood up and threw away the last of the paper towels. "I'm going to go now," she said quietly. There was nothing more to say. It wasn't as if her mother was going to embrace her and squeal with joy at the thought of grandchildren. So the lump of disappointment in her throat was useless. She turned and walked toward the door.

"Lainey—wait."

She paused and turned.

Jacqui asked, "Who else knows about this?"

Lainey laid her hand on her belly and saw Jacqui flinch. "Only Beth knows about your grandchild." There wasn't any reason to tell her Ben knew as well. It would only make things worse.

"Okay, good. We need to make this spin positive somehow. I'll get on it and let you know the plan." Jacqui, clearly perked by the thought of something to do, padded across the carpet on sticky feet.

"No."

Jacqui stopped. "Excuse me?"

Lainey shook her head. "You can plan all you want, but it's not going to make it go away. Not going to make it any more or less than it is. I'm not going to go along with any plan. My baby. My life."

Jacqui's mouth flattened. "Your store—"

"I know. It's at your mercy." Lainey grabbed her purse. "You keep telling me. Now you know why I won't let it go under. I need to succeed so I can support myself and my child. Can I call anyone for you before I go?"

Jacqui shook her head. "No. I don't—I need to talk to your father first. He's going to be so disappointed," she added, more to herself than to Lainey. "Plus it's an election year."

Lainey stared at her. "Mom, I'm thirty-three. Not a teenager. Not even close. So what if I have a baby on my own?" She nearly laughed. As if it was such an easy thing to do. Maybe she was crazy. "Women do it all the time."

"But not women in *your* position," Jacqui said.

She kept her voice steady with effort. "And what position would that be?"

"Women whose lives are under scrutiny," she said, and Lainey's jaw nearly dropped.

"I'm hardly under any kind of scrutiny. Besides, I don't think this is any worse than my divorce," she said dryly. "And it's a much happier occasion."

Jacqui shook her head. "Don't make a joke of it. You don't understand. You never have."

Lainey hesitated, then simply turned and walked toward the door. There wasn't anything else to say. Behind her, she heard her mother on the phone with the housekeeper, telling her to come clean up the mess.

Outside, she took a deep breath as she got in her car and drove out of the driveway. Then she pulled over. She reached for her cell and called her brother.

Amazingly, Kevin answered.

"You're not in surgery today?"

"Nope. Office visits all day. I've only got a few minutes, though. What's up?"

Lainey fiddled with the steering wheel. "I just came from home."

"Oh? How's Mom?"

Lainey stared out the window, not seeing the rain on the windshield. "I kind of shocked her, Kev. She's not happy."

"You told her you're pregnant?"

Tears stung her eyes. Even though she'd suspected he knew. "How did you know?"

He sighed. "I can just tell. Where are you going for your OB?"

Lainey filled him in on the details.

"Is Lawless the father?"

Oh, she wished. Of the few men she'd been involved with, he was the most honorable, hands down. "No," she whispered.

He made a noise that could have been anything. "I caught him looking at you a couple times on Saturday. Really looking. Not how a brother wants a guy to look at his kid sister."

She nearly laughed, and tried to ignore the spurt of pleasure and pain his words caused. "Wow. I'm pretty sure you're wrong. And don't ask me any more about the father, okay? It's not—he's not interested in being a father."

"That's too damn bad," he growled. "Do you need me to hunt him down?"

Now she *did* laugh, at the vision of her respectable surgeon older brother beating the hell out of Jon. It would be quite a match, but her money would be on Kevin. "No. But, thanks."

A pause. "That's not right, Lainey. He shouldn't leave you—"

"It's okay," she interrupted him. "We're better off without him."

Kevin sighed. "All right. And, little sis? You'll be a hell of a mother."

His words and his faith in her warmed her. It was so nice to have him stand up for her. But still… "I don't want to be like our mother," she whispered. There it was…her deepest fear.

Kevin snorted. "You won't be. She somehow flat-out missed the maternal gene. You've got it in spades. You feeling okay?"

"Yeah. Just a little tired. Thankfully I don't have much nausea."

"Okay, good. I've got to run. I'll stop by and see Mom after I get out of here. Let me know if I can help, okay? You don't have to do this alone."

His words brought tears to her eyes. "Thanks, Kev. I will," she promised, and disconnected, feeling a little better. Kevin would smooth out what Lainey couldn't, but she doubted either of them could make Jacqui see this as a good thing.

She tucked the phone back into her purse and sat for another few moments. Her mother's reaction hadn't really shocked her. Jacqui would spin and spin, but in the end it was what Lainey did that mattered, and she'd make it work on her own. Again, if things were different— But they weren't. Whatever was going on with Ben, it had him clearly reluctant to make even the slightest commitment. She needed someone reliable.

So far the only reliable one was herself. The irony of that wasn't lost on her.

Lainey stood in her new backyard the next day after work and stared up into the nearly empty oak tree, then down at the ground where she stood ankle deep in yellow-brown leaves. Yesterday they'd all been on the tree. Today they were all on the ground. Clearly it was time for a trip to the hardware store to buy a rake.

She trudged through the leaves, hearing the crunch under her feet, on her way out front to her car. Her trip to the hardware store, where she purchased a rake, leaf bags, and a pair of work gloves, took less than half an hour.

She went out back, rake in hand, and tilted her face to the sun. She had a couple of hours before it would be too dark. Might as well make the most of it.

She hadn't been going for more than ten minutes when Ben's big truck pulled in the driveway. Her pulse kicked up and she gripped the rake a little harder. She walked over to the gate to greet him.

"Hi," she said, when he emerged from the truck and turned her way. She tried not to devour him with her eyes. She wanted to curl herself into his embrace, feel his warmth through the black fleece jacket he wore—

Wait. No, she didn't.

"Hey," he said, coming closer, his expression neutral. His gaze dropped to her belly. "Is this okay, in your condition?"

"Of course. I'm not doing any heavy lifting, so I'm fine," she said. "I can do pretty much anything as long as I don't overdo it."

He lifted his gaze to hers. "I can see you overdoing it."

She smiled and shook her head. "I'm very careful. I'm not going to put the baby in any danger."

"Of course you won't. I'll help."

She tried not to stare at the rear view as he walked to the bed of his truck. How could she not notice how those worn jeans hugged his rear and thighs just right? She cleared her throat. "Do you just carry a rake in the back of your truck for emergencies?"

"I was here earlier and saw what had happened," he answered as she stepped aside for him to come through the gate. Before she could ask, he nodded to the garage. "The light in there was out. I put in a new bulb."

"I'm going to get spoiled—all this personal landlord service," she teased, and saw his back stiffen. "Not to worry. I can change my own lightbulbs."

He sent her a grin. "Does your mother know?"

"Shh," she murmured. "She'll hear you."

He laughed and started raking.

They worked in relative silence for a bit. Lainey kept sneaking glances at him. He'd unzipped his jacket and, while the tee shirt he wore underneath wasn't exactly skin-tight, she could still see the play of muscles underneath it when he raked.

She exhaled. It had certainly gotten hotter out here since he had shown up.

They raked a big pile over the next little while, and a slight breeze stirred the remaining leaves on the tree and several came floating down. He reached out and plucked a piece of one out of her hair, his fingers lingering on the strands. Her mouth went dry at the intense heat in his gaze and her pulse kicked up when he dropped his gaze to her mouth. Lainey stopped herself from leaning forward, from pressing her mouth to his. He stepped back and offered her the leaf with a small smile.

She took it and twirled the stem in her fingers. "Wow, thanks." She held it up, looking at the red and green threaded in with the yellow. "Pretty, isn't it?"

He closed his hand over hers. She looked up into his gaze.

"Gorgeous," he murmured, drawing her closer and she knew, with a flutter deep inside, that he wasn't talking about the leaf anymore.

He settled his mouth over hers. With a sigh,

she melted into him, opening, letting his tongue slip in. When the kiss became deeper, hotter, she fisted the front of his jacket and he gripped her hips, drawing her closer, before plunging one hand into her hair, angling her head to thrust his tongue even deeper.

Fire skipped through her veins, burned along her nerve-endings, sent heat arrowing into the depth of her belly. She pressed closer, feeling his hardness against her and the answering heat of her response.

Suddenly he broke the kiss, though he didn't pull away from her, but rested his forehead on hers. Their breath mingled as she tried to calm her breathing. Every time he touched her she craved more. It wasn't enough. But it was all there was. Frustration welled and she squeezed her eyes shut.

"Lainey," he murmured, his voice raw and rough. "I told myself I'd stay away, but..." His voice trailed off as he stepped back, and she shivered from the loss of his heat. "We'd better get to work."

Shaking, Lainey bent to retrieve her discarded

rake. She needed to pull back, keep this kind of thing from happening.

But the real question was, did she want to? In her heart, she feared the answer was no.

CHAPTER NINE

IT DIDN'T TAKE all that long to make a huge pile. Ben pulled some sticks out. "When was the last time you jumped in a leaf pile?"

Shame flushed Lainey's cheeks. "Well, never."

He stared at her. "No way? All those trees on your parents' land and you never played in a leaf pile?"

"No. My mother—you'd have to know my mother. She's not big on dirt." That sounded sad, but it was the truth.

"Oh." There was a wealth of understanding in the word. "I see."

She looked at him in surprise. "You do?"

He nodded. "You need to experience it before the baby gets here. Let me make sure all the sticks are out."

He poked in the pile and she watched with a combination of amusement and exasperation. After extracting a few more sticks, he fluffed the pile with his rake and turned, the satisfaction on his face making her laugh.

"Does it pass muster?" she teased gently.

He nodded. "You're not too far along for this, are you?"

On impulse, Lainey unzipped her vest and ran her hand over her very slight baby bump. The tenderness in his eyes as he watched made her breath catch. "Am I jumping out of a tree?"

His gaze jerked up. "Of course not."

"Then I'll be fine." She leapt lightly into the pile, landing on her knees. The crackle of the leaves and their fresh scent invigorated her. She laughed and threw an armful of leaves in the air, then tried to cover her head when they came raining back down.

"Incoming!" Ben called, and before she could scramble too far over he came crashing into the pile with her. He gave her a big grin—the first she'd seen with no shadows, no pain in his eyes—and tossed a handful of leaves at her. "So, what do you think?"

She threw some back at him. "It was worth the wait."

He laughed. "Yeah? Awesome." He turned and

flopped back, folding his hands under his head. "I'm guessing you never looked at cloud shapes either?"

"Stop reminding me how deprived my childhood was," she scolded him with a laugh, and he snaked out a hand and pulled her head down to his. The sweetness of this kiss after the passion of the earlier one threw her.

When she pulled back, searching his face with her gaze, he touched her cheek, twining his fingers in her hair. "I'm sorry," he said.

She arched a brow. "For what?"

"For all you missed. I assumed, growing up as you did, you had everything."

She shrugged and pulled a leaf out of his hair. "I had everything material you could want. Only I didn't actually want it. I didn't get time with my parents. But I see now my mom didn't know how to raise us. She was so caught up in perceptions that just letting me be a kid wasn't possible. She meant well, but..." She sat up in the leaves. "We turned out okay, Kevin and I. Him more than me," she added with a little sigh, thinking of her struggling shop, her pregnancy and her money woes.

Ben frowned. "Don't do that."

Startled, she looked at him. "Do what?"

"Put yourself down like that. You're living life on your terms. How is that not okay?"

"Oh." She nibbled on her lip while she thought. "You're right. I hadn't thought of it like that. I guess I just want to prove I can do it."

"You are. You will." He stood up and extended a hand to her.

His quiet confidence warmed her down to her toes and her heart tipped dangerously.

"Let's get this done."

She grasped his warm, callused palm and let him draw her to her feet. "Okay."

They managed to load about half the leaves into bags before it got too dark. Lainey's arms and back were screaming, and it was with an incredible sense of relief that she dropped her rake on the ground to stretch her back.

"Did you overdo it?" The concern in his voice made her smile.

"According to my back and arms, yes. But none of that will hurt the baby."

"Go on in," he told her. "I'll put these things in the garage. I'll finish tomorrow."

She hesitated before starting toward the house. "Do you—do you want to come in? For coffee or something?"

"I'd like that," he said softly. "If you think you aren't too tired?"

"No, I'm fine. Come in when you're done."

She hurried into the house and started the coffee maker. A quick trip to the bathroom revealed wild hair and a nose bright red from the cold.

Oooh. Sexy.

Though Ben clearly hadn't minded. He'd kissed her. Twice.

Would there be a third time?

She shook her head at her reflection. *Stop it.* She detoured to the living room to switch on the fire. While the walls were bare in here, as she hadn't had a chance yet to deal with artwork, she'd gotten the furniture arranged like she wanted and unpacked pillows and a couple throws. It was comfy enough for the moment. Ben would understand.

When she got back to the kitchen she caught a glimpse of him coming out of the garage. For just a heartbeat she was a wife and a mom, waiting for her man to come in.

The thought threw her. She'd been a wife, and had given up waiting for her man to come in pretty quickly. She was going to be a mom—and that terrified her. But she'd never felt for her ex-husband what she felt for Ben—and she wasn't even in love with Ben.

Not yet.

Reeling from that thought, she opened the cupboard to take out coffee mugs as Ben came in through the back door. She gave him a bright smile. "It's decaf. That okay?"

"Sure," he said, and shrugged out of his jacket.

She poured his and handed it to him. "Let's go in here," she said and led the way to the living room. She settled on the couch with him across from her.

"Something wrong? You look a little pale."

Ben's casual comment threw her. She certainly couldn't tell him *he* was part of what was worrying her. "I'm not ready to be a mother," she blurted. "But I'm committed now."

He looked genuinely surprised. "Why do you think you're not ready?"

"I'm still getting my shop off the ground. I'm not in the best place financially." He just looked at her and she shut her eyes. "I'm not. My parents are wealthy, yes, but there was no trust fund or anything. It was kind of understood I'd either get a fantastic career or a loaded husband. Or both." She stared at his shoulder, unable to meet his eyes. "I managed to do neither."

"You say that like it's a bad thing," he said softly.

She looked at him and the misery in her eyes nearly had him reaching for her. He wanted to tuck her under his arm and hold her against his chest, where he already knew she fit perfectly.

"I know it shouldn't be. And my ex-husband is a real doozy. Seven years of my life I'll never get back. But somehow it is—in my family. I'm happy where I am. I'm just—"

She stopped and he saw the sheen of tears. "Just what?"

"So worried. Because I don't want to be a bad mother," Lainey blurted, and covered her face with her hands.

Now he did reach for her, and caught her wrists and gently pulled her hands away. "Why would you think you would be?"

She gave a harsh little laugh and looked down

in her lap. "My mother has no maternal genes. None. Zero. We aren't close, even though it seems like I see her all the time. I don't want my baby to feel like he or she doesn't matter."

Anger washed through him. "You feel like you don't matter?"

She stood up and walked over to the fireplace. She stared into the dancing flames. "I— Yes. I've never really been a part of the family. I always felt like just a prop, I guess. The black sheep."

He came up behind her and slid his hands down her arms. "You are going to be a wonderful mother, Lainey." When she shook her head, he leaned down and pressed his cheek to hers, inhaled her sweet scent. "Listen to me. I haven't known you long, but what I see is a warm, compassionate, giving woman who cares deeply about those who matter to her. You're strong. You're sweet. You're funny. All of that is going to translate naturally to motherhood."

She turned in his arms and looked up at him, her eyes huge in the soft light of the lamp and the fire. The uncertainty in her eyes killed him.

"You think so?"

He'd meant every word. He touched her face,

unable to stop himself from feeling her soft skin. She leaned into him just slightly, eyes closed, and he swallowed hard but couldn't step away even if he wanted to. Which, God help him, he didn't.

"No. I know so."

Her eyes fluttered open and he gave in, lowering his mouth to hers, hearing her sharp inhale. He hesitated at the last second. Her breath feathered over his and she closed the gap, coming up to meet him. He slipped his hands in her hair, even though they really wanted to roam farther south. All he wanted to do right now was feel.

Lainey. Only Lainey.

The kiss grew more urgent quickly, and she opened to him with a little growl in her throat that only served to fuel his internal fire. When her arms went around his neck and she pressed her length against him he was lost.

No. He was found. He hadn't wanted to be, and he wouldn't be able to stay. But she'd managed to lay waste to all his defenses.

He broke the kiss before he accidentally toppled her into the fireplace and rested his forehead on hers. She didn't move away, though he felt the tension return to her body. "I didn't want you to end up in the fire."

She blinked at him, then a small smile curved her mouth. "Thoughtful of you."

"Isn't it, though? Gentleman through and through." He savored her laugh as he took her hand and led her to the couch. If she knew how badly he wanted to take her to bed, to feel her move beneath him, to make love to her, she'd know he wasn't any kind of gentleman.

And those thoughts weren't helpful.

Trying to bring them back around, he asked, "How are your shoulders?"

She rolled them and winced. "I'll be feeling this for a couple days, I think."

He pulled her down on the couch and sat so he was behind her. He began to knead her shoulders gently. "Wow. You *are* tight. Relax and let me see if I can help with that."

She let her head fall forward. "Mmm. That feels wonderful."

Yeah. It did. But touching her like this, on top of the kisses earlier, was sending all his blood south. And when she moaned his breath shortened. He leaned forward and kissed her neck, still massaging, but letting his hands slip over her shoulders to brush the tops of her breasts through her shirt, then moving them back up to her shoulders. Her little inhale prompted him to do it again, this time slipping his hands under her breasts to cup them in his hands, brush his thumbs over her nipples. Was this one of the lacy, sexy bras he'd seen that day in her bathroom?

"Lainey…" he murmured against her neck, and she tilted her head to the side, her breathing shallow. He kissed her neck one more time and she shifted out of his arms. He let her go, instantly feeling her loss, but she just turned around and settled on his lap, wrapped her arms around his neck.

"Stay," she whispered. "Please."

"Lainey." He rested his forehead on hers, struggling for some semblance of control. "Are you sure?"

She slid off his lap and held out her hand. It was trembling slightly and he could see uncertainty warring with desire in her eyes. She was offering him a gift and she was afraid he wouldn't take it.

This might be his only chance. A few hours of heaven he knew he didn't deserve.

But Lainey did.

He took her hand without ever breaking eye contact and stood.

Smoke filled the room, smothering him, searing his lungs, his eyes, his skin. God, he couldn't see through the gray haze. A cough racked him, tearing at his parched throat. He couldn't yell for his friend. Where was Jason? He couldn't reach him—had to get him out before the house came down around him. A roar and a crack, and orange lit the room. The ceiling caved in on a crash fueled by the roar of flames. He spun around, but the door was blocked by a flaming heap of debris. Under it was a boot. Jason coming to save him.

Ben woke up, gasping, to find Lainey's terrified face over him.

"Ben?"

The concern, the worry, was too much for him, and he clamped both hands over his face so she couldn't see the pain, the anger, the shame seeping from him like tears.

Her hand was soft on his arm. "Ben?"

He shook her off. "Lainey—don't. God. I—it's

just a dream." He sat up, cursing himself for falling asleep, for allowing the intimacy at all, for thinking maybe it would be okay.

She drew back, a sheet pulled up over those glorious breasts, her gaze steady and worried. "If it's just a dream why are you so rattled?"

She saw too much. Too damn much. He was stripped emotionally bare after their wonderful night together—all that emotion which he hadn't expected.

"I can't explain it now," he said, weary. "Go back to sleep. I'll see myself out."

Her quick intake of breath lanced him. No point in telling her he wouldn't sleep anymore, anyway. Better she knew as little as possible. Better he didn't give her the chance to soothe him, to connect, while he was vulnerable.

She said nothing as he pulled on his pants in the dark, fumbled with his wallet.

"What ever it is, running isn't going to make it go away."

Her words, though soft, hit him as hard as if she'd shouted or thrown glass shards at him.

"It's not going to make it stop."

"I'm sorry," was all he could say, while he

thought, *Yeah, but all I can do is run.* If she knew what he'd done she'd never speak to him again. Bad enough now she'd see him as weak.

He paused in the doorway, looked back. She'd lain down again, her back to the door, covers pulled all the way up. He ached to go back to her, but he knew it was for the best.

"Go if you're going to," she said, her voice raw, and he did, leaving her in her warm bed and slipping into the chilly night.

Beth stopped in her tracks as soon as she entered the shop the next morning. "Wow. You look tired. What happened?"

Lainey winced, then sighed. It was true. Between Ben keeping her awake and then leaving after the nightmare she'd gotten pretty much no sleep. "Ben happened."

Beth cocked her head. "If you were glowing, I'd guess the lack of sleep was due to happy times with Ben," she said. "But I'm guessing not so much?"

"It ended badly," Lainey said finally. "I'm not sure what happened. We were—well, we…" She paused as her cheeks heated and Beth's brow rose as a grin stole across her face. "I guess I don't have to explain it to you. But he just left." She shrugged as if it hadn't hurt. After how wonderful everything had been, she couldn't *help* but be hurt.

It infuriated her.

"Just walked out as in thanks and bye?" Beth's tone was incredulous.

"Not quite that crass, but, yeah." Lainey couldn't tell Beth about Ben's nightmare. He seemed to be ashamed of it, and it wasn't her place to tell anyone. "I really don't want to talk about it."

Beth sent her a sympathetic look. "Love is messy."

Lainey nearly dropped the bucket she held. No one had said anything about love. Especially not with a man who was clearly keeping something from her. "We've just got really good chemistry."

"Chemistry is good," Beth said cheerfully. "And, all told, this is a huge improvement over last week, when I told you to go for it and you looked like I'd kicked a puppy." Her voice sobered and she threw an arm around Lainey's shoulders. "Seriously, though, I see more than just chemistry. The way you say his name—"

"Oh, Beth." Lainey interrupted before this got any worse. "I do *not*. Obviously I like him a lot but that's all. There's no more than that."

Except the slight twist in her belly told a different story. The way he'd loved her, cherished her. The way he made her feel important. The way he stood up for her, even to herself. How crushed she'd been when he shut her out last night.

Oh, no.

Beth looked at her steadily. "If you say so."

Lainey forced a smile. "I do say so." As she forced herself to walk casually to the back room, gripping the bucket handle so hard it hurt, she was afraid Beth was right. This whole thing, at least for her, had tipped well past mutual chemistry and into dangerous emotional territory.

Clearly she'd learned nothing from her past.

But Ben wasn't Daniel or Jon. And, really, how would she know love? She'd never been in love before. It most certainly couldn't happen this quickly.

Could it?

* * *

Ben sat at the Rusty Hammer bar, a burger with all the trimmings before him. Best damn burgers anywhere, but it could be cardboard for all he could taste it. Still, the owner was looking at him, so he gave it a shot.

Someone settled on the bar stool next to him. A quick glance revealed Kevin Keeler. The other man nodded in acknowledgement and Ben did the same. Fantastic. Just what he needed.

"What can I get you?" The owner had come to stand in front of Kevin.

Kevin inclined his head toward Ben's plate. "One of those and a beer, please."

"On the way." He drew the beer, placed it in front of Kevin and headed for the kitchen.

Kevin took a long draw. He set the glass down with a thunk and half turned to Ben, who braced himself.

"So. What are your intentions toward my sister?"

Ben nearly choked on his burger. Kevin thumped him on the back. "It's probably a good idea to do that in front of a doctor," he observed dryly.

Ben shook his head and grabbed his beer. Was this a trick question? Did Kevin know he'd slept with her? He doubted it. Lainey would never kiss and tell to Kevin. Besides, big brothers weren't inclined to be friendly when you messed with their little sisters.

"Nothing. No intentions. She needed a date and invited me to the gala. That's all." His words were hollow but he hoped Kevin wouldn't pick up on it. He'd never intended anything to go as far as it had, physically or otherwise. She'd filled holes in him that had desperately needed filling, as hard as he'd tried to avoid it.

Kevin tapped his glass. "It doesn't look like *all*," he said. "You were looking at her pretty seriously. With her being pregnant, I need to know what your intentions are."

Ben picked up his beer and took a deliberate swallow. "Like I said—"

Kevin leaned in. "She deserves better than a guy with *no intentions*. A hell of a lot better. She's been through hell and back with that idiot of an ex-husband, not to mention our selfish, clueless parents."

Ben met the other man's serious gaze. "I completely agree. That's why I have no intention of getting tangled up in her life." *Anymore than I already am.* "She asked for a favor. I agreed. She's an amazing woman and I wish her all the best."

Kevin sat back with a frown. "She's got feelings for you."

"I hope not," he said quietly, but he knew Kevin was right. The hell of it was, he had powerful feelings for her, too. "Like I said, I can't give her what she needs." The truth was painful and he gripped the bottle tighter. "So. My intentions are to walk away and let her live her life." The words were like ash in his mouth.

Kevin nodded at the owner, who'd delivered his burger. "I'm not sure if you're smart or a coward."

Ben barked out a laugh. "Truthfully? Me either."

Actually, that wasn't true. He did know. He was keeping Lainey safe, and that wasn't a cowardly move.

Was it?

For all his not wanting to be part of a family, for not wanting home and hearth and kids and a wife, he knew underneath it all he was a sham. He wanted all of it. He wanted what Jason and

Callie had had. He didn't know how to open himself up to have it. But if he could— Lainey was a good woman. She'd be a wonderful mother and wife to the right man.

Just not for him.

CHAPTER TEN

LAINEY HURRIED HOME after work on the day of the gala. Of course her mother *would* schedule this party on a Thursday. And, being only her and Beth at the shop, Lainey couldn't exactly take the afternoon off. So she was left with an hour to do all the primping required for a black tie affair.

Her nerves wouldn't settle. She hadn't seen Ben since he'd left that night. She took a deep breath and tried to focus on her hair and make-up, which were thankfully simple. Even with a redo of eyeliner due to her shaking hand. She got the dress on and tried to suck in her belly as she turned to study herself in the full-length mirror. Then she relaxed. The black fabric draped low over her breasts and gathered gently at her stomach, so the pregnancy wasn't obvious.

She eyed the black heels lying on the floor of her room. Sparkly and sexy, they absolutely killed her feet.

She'd make the sacrifice.

The doorbell rang and she scooped up the shoes and made a quick stop in the bathroom. She tried to examine her make-up in the mirror, but all she could see was flushed cheeks and sparkling eyes. She'd piled her hair on her head in an elaborate updo the likes of which she didn't have a reason for too often anymore.

For someone who'd insisted repeatedly this night meant nothing, she'd sure spent a lot of energy stressing over it.

Hearing the bell again, she took a deep breath and hurried over to open the door.

She simply lost her breath.

The tux emphasized Ben's broad shoulders and slim hips. His hair curled a little over the collar, and she took a step back so she didn't reach out to run her fingers through it.

His gaze swept over her in the way a man's did when he appreciated a woman he was interested in. Her nerve-endings sizzled, as if he'd actually caressed her. Heat ran down her spine and he gave her a rare, slow smile.

"You're gorgeous." The words were simple, heartfelt, and she felt her heart stutter at the raw edge in his tone. Daniel had never looked at her like that or said anything so simple—and meant it. Something inside her shifted.

"Thank you," she managed. "So are you."

She stepped aside to let him in. The butterflies in her stomach had grown into bats.

She cleared her throat. "I've just got to get my shoes on."

"All right." He studied her while she sat down and buckled them on her feet. When she stood he must have noticed her wince. "Why do you wear them if they hurt?"

No point in being cagey. "They look great." She lifted the hem of her dress over her ankle so he could see. "See?"

He lifted his gaze from her ankle to her face and she felt the heat of it. She was very glad she'd decided to paint her toenails a sexy red.

An answering sizzle ran through her as he cleared his throat. "Lovely." His voice was still a bit hoarse.

A visceral shudder ran through her at the memory of his hands on her the other night. How wonderful they'd been together. Until he'd left.

She swallowed and grabbed her clutch. "I'm ready."

He rested his hand on the small of her back as they went out her door. The touch was familiar and intimate. "What do women carry in those things anyway?"

"This?" Lainey held up the silver clutch. At his nod she continued. "Well, I've got keys, phone, lipstick, a couple of tissues. A couple of make-up things. The usual girl stuff, I guess." Other than things like tampons, of course. Pregnant girls didn't need those.

"Keys? In there?" He stepped aside so she could lock the door.

"Well, off the ring. Just for the door— Oh!" She turned around and stared at the black coupe, an exact replica of the one she'd owned a year ago. Daniel's gift to her. Recovering before he could notice her shock, she added, "Nice ride."

"Thanks." He opened the door for her and held it while she got in. The rich scent of the buttery leather and the new carpet hit her. A few seconds later he was sliding in the driver's seat. "I didn't think my usual ride was appropriate for tonight.

I figured you'd be in a fancy dress and it might be hard to climb in and out of the truck."

Her heart caught. He'd done it for her. Even though she'd ambushed him with it less than two weeks ago, he'd come through. "Thank you," she said after she got her voice back. "It was very thoughtful of you."

"More what you're used to," he said, without looking at her.

Oh, so *that* was how it was. "Ben, you see what I drive now."

He said nothing and she sighed. "It's in my past. And I'm happier without it." The full truth there. That car had symbolized her ultimate failure and catalyzed her ability to do something about it. She gave the dashboard an affectionate little pat and heard Ben's low chuckle.

The full moon hung huge and silver in the obsidian sky as they drove to the Lakeside Country Club. As she looked at it, shining over the lake, she couldn't help but wonder if her mother had managed to call in a favor from somewhere to arrange for the moon.

The club, of course, was gorgeous. What had to be miles of twinkle lights outlined the building, luminaries lined the walkways, and through the wide glass doors she could see a roaring fire in the fireplace. Ben pulled up to the port-cochere and a valet glided forward to open the door. "Good evening, sir and madam," he said as Ben held his hand out and helped Lainey out of the car. She was perfectly capable of exiting on her own, but with Ben it didn't feel like a grand gesture for the sake of it but more as if he wanted to touch her any way he could.

So she let him.

The valet closed the door and took Ben's keys. He cocked his arm at her. "Shall we?"

She tucked her hand in the warm crook of his arm and enjoyed the little fizzy feeling touching him gave her. She took a deep breath and had to keep herself from turning into him to just breathe him in. "Yes. Let's."

After stepping inside and taking care of her wrap, Lainey proceeded with Ben to the hall where the gala was being held. It was early, so the room was little more than half full, and they perused the tables until they found theirs. With her parents, of course. And Kevin.

"Lot of people here already," Ben commented, looking around.

"Yes," Lainey agreed. "Mother does a wonderful job with this." Credit where it was due. Her mother knew how to throw a party.

Lainey spotted her mother heading toward them, a vision in designer gold. On anyone else the form-fitting gown would be tacky. On Jacqui it was perfect.

"Lainey." She offered her cheek and Lainey dutifully kissed her, then offered her own.

"Hi, Mother." She laid a hand on Ben's arm, felt the heat of him through his sleeve. "This is Ben Lawless. Ben, this is my mother—Jacqui Keeler."

Jacqui gave Ben an obvious once-over. He held out his hand with a smile and she took it.

"Nice to meet you," he said.

"Likewise," she said, and turned to Lainey. "Now, honey, you two mingle for a bit before you take your seats. And no leaving until ten o'clock." Someone must have signaled her mother, because Jacqui turned abruptly to leave before Lainey could say a word. "I'll see you at dinner." And she was gone.

"Sorry," Lainey said immediately. "My mom's

a little intense. Don't take it personally." What Jacqui could find lacking in the smoking hot package that was Ben, Lainey couldn't fathom. Because he wasn't Daniel? Couldn't give her what her mother deemed most important—money?

"I see that," Ben said as he steered her toward a buffet table piled high with sinful goodies. "And I'm not offended. Let's get something to drink."

Along the way they got pulled into several conversations—people who knew Lainey, or thought they did. The whole process was as exhausting as it always had been to smile for her mother or stump for her father. Tonight was a bit of both.

"Here." Ben pushed a golden flute into her hand. "I know your...situation. But I think you need this. Just carry it if nothing else."

The champagne bubbled in the flute and Lainey took a tiny sip. It fizzed in her mouth and slid down her throat. Ben was right. Just having it in her hand was enough. She didn't need anyone questioning why she refused to drink. "Thank you. It hits the spot."

Ben bent so his mouth was next to her ear. She could hear him over the band, which had just started up. "You're welcome."

Lainey hoped he didn't notice the little shiver that skittered down her spine at his warm breath on her skin. She was so, so lost to this man. And he didn't even know it.

He moved away slightly and she felt the immediate loss of contact. She chided herself for letting herself get caught up in this even for a moment. Despite her decision to enjoy tonight, it wasn't real. It didn't change anything.

"So, what's good here?" Ben asked her as they surveyed the table loaded with *hors d'oeuvres* of every persuasion. There were tiny *petit-fours*, as well as fancy little things that looked like shrimp, mushrooms, cheese. All high end. No mini hot dogs for this party.

"I'd say all of it," she said. "My mother doesn't skimp on this stuff."

He smiled and handed her a plate. "Not surprised."

Lainey took a few small things and put them on her plate, and Ben did the same. Her brother approached them and Lainey braced herself.

"Laine," Kevin greeted her. She noticed he was dateless, and frowned.

"Kev, where's your date? How did *you* get away

with coming stag?" Realizing how her words sounded, she quickly turned to Ben.

He just nodded at Kevin and said, "I see someone I need to talk to. I'll catch up with you in a bit, okay?"

"Um, okay," Lainey said, feeling like a total heel.

"Nice job," Kevin commented, lifting a flute of champagne from a passing waiter. "You've got a way with men, sis."

Lainey sent him a sour look, even though he was right. "I didn't mean it how it sounded." Still, she'd hurt Ben with her thoughtless comment. And after he'd gone to such trouble for her tonight. She tracked him with her eyes and noticed he'd stopped next to a tall, gorgeous, slender blond. Who couldn't possibly have natural boobs. Lainey frowned.

"And you're not listening to anything I say," Kevin said, amusement in his tone. "You can't take your eyes off the guy, can you? Does Mother know?"

"Does Mother know what?" Jacqui materialized next to them and peered critically at Lainey's plate. "Be careful, dear. I know you're—" she glanced around and lowered her voice "—pregnant, but you don't want to gain a lot of weight."

Lainey looked at her and for the first time saw an unhappy, brittle woman whose need to control everything had nearly estranged her from her children and whose marriage had taken a serious toll on her self-worth. Instead of being insulted by her thoughtless words, Lainey felt only pity.

"No worries, Mother," she said smoothly, and selected a prosciutto something from her plate. She was eating for two, right? Might as well do it tonight. "Lovely party, by the way."

Effectively sidetracked, Jacqui glowed. "It is, isn't it? Almost time to get seated for dinner. Lainey, get your date. Kevin, thanks for coming. I know you have to get back later."

Lainey's gaze lasered to Ben as her mother hurried off. Now he was laughing with the blond, his dark head near her golden one. Something sour curled in her belly. Couldn't be jealousy, could it? Despite their night together, and all her feelings for him, she had no actual claim on him. None at all.

So it was silly and petty to be jealous.

As if he'd felt her watching him, he lifted his

head and locked on her gaze. The sour feeling was replaced by something much, much sweeter.

Kevin stepped closer, into her line of sight, his gaze intense and knowing. Her stomach sank.

"Anything you want to tell me, sis?"

Lainey stared up at him. *Oh, no.* She swallowed hard. "No. Nothing."

He gave a little nod and stepped back. He looked as if he wanted to say something, then thought better of it and turned and walked away.

Ben made his way through the crowd to Lainey. Her gaze snapped to his and relief lit her big blue eyes just for a moment. Then it was gone.

"Sorry about that," Ben said, coming up next to her. She smelled so good. Like vanilla and something sinful. Sweet and sinful. That was Lainey, all wrapped up in one sexy package.

Sexy *pregnant* package, that was.

God, he was in trouble.

"It's okay." Her voice was a little remote. "Of course you know people here."

"Megan is an old friend, but not *that* kind of friend." Ben surprised himself by how important it was that she understand. "I was surprised to see her here."

She gave him a sideways look. "I get it."

He caught her hand and twined his fingers with hers. She looked down, clearly startled, then up to his face.

"Lainey. You are the only woman I can see." The words were rough in his throat, but true in every sense. There was no one but her. If things were different there would never be anyone but her. All he could give her was tonight. It had to be enough.

Her gaze stayed on his, her blue eyes wide and hopeful, fearful. He wanted to drown in them, in her. Instead he gave her fingers a squeeze and stepped back. "I take it we're supposed to sit down?"

A shadow passed over her face quickly, then she smiled. "Shall we?"

They made their way to the table. He noted she kept an eye on her parents, who were still mingling and mixing and chatting up the guests. The table was set for eight and Kevin was already there, his gaze firmly on Ben.

His words from the other night hit him hard.

No intentions. Yeah, he was a liar. He wanted so much more than he could give her—wanted to give her what she deserved—and Kevin's hard stare said he knew it. Not only that, he knew Ben was going to walk. Ben met the other man's gaze squarely. They both knew she deserved better.

Dinner went fairly quickly. Prime rib, decadent desserts, rich sides all filled the plates. Ben hadn't eaten so well in ages. Lainey, he noted, only picked at her food.

"Not hungry?"

She looked up and flushed. "Not really. These things—it's not my cup of tea." She slid her plate toward him. "Here. Help yourself if you want."

He did fork up a couple of pieces of her prime rib, because it *was* prime rib and he was a guy. He caught Jacqui's fierce frown at her daughter as she got up and he wondered at it.

Jacqui walked to the microphone at the front of the room. After a little speech of welcome and thanks, she added, "Dancing will begin as soon as the last of the plates are cleared. Don't forget the silent auction—there's still time to place your bids."

"I'm going to hit the ladies' room," Lainey

murmured to him. She stood and picked up her little silver purse. "Back in a few."

"So. Ben." Her father leaned forward across the table as soon as Lainey had left. "How do you know my daughter?"

Wow, was he sixteen again, or what? He kept his tone level. "Through my grandmother. Lainey's been helping her out at her place."

The man looked surprised. "Really?"

Ben nodded. "I think her visits are the highlight of Grandma's week." How could this guy not know the kind of person his daughter was?

"What do you do for a living?"

Ben tensed just slightly. This man could and would ferret out the truth, and Ben would bet he wanted to know. "I'm a firefighter."

Greg Keeler arched a brow. "Really? Where?"

"City of Grand Rapids." He hesitated for a beat as he met the other man's gaze. "I'm on medical leave right now." Better just to say it than have it found out and used against Lainey somehow.

The very fact he was even concerned was a problem.

The older man's gaze sharpened. It was no doubt only a matter of time before the man looked him up if he thought Ben was interested in his daughter. "I hope your recovery is going well."

Ben managed a smile. "Well enough." Actually, there was some truth to that. Being around Lainey had helped him. Better than any therapy.

Greg leaned across the table. "While being a firefighter is a very important job, you need to realize you're not what we have in mind for Lainey," he said, almost apologetically. "Her ex-husband is a partner in a very prestigious law firm. I understand they're considering reconciliation."

Ben's brow shot up, as did his pulse. He sure as hell hadn't seen any indication that Lainey was interested in her ex-husband. In fact, if memory served him, she was no fan of his. "Is that so? Then why isn't he here with her?"

"Because I didn't invite him." Lainey's voice was cold as she stood behind Ben and regarded her father with sharp eyes. "He's my ex-husband for a lot of very good reasons."

Her father sat back and shook his head. "Lainey—"

She shot him a hard look and turned to Ben as the band struck up. "Want to dance?"

"Of course." He pushed back from the table and inclined his head to Greg. The older man crossed his arms and frowned as he led Lainey away.

"How about a walk instead?" he asked. The band was playing, but it was too early to dance. They'd be the only ones on the floor, and possibly the center of attention. He doubted Lainey wanted that.

She nodded. "I'd like that."

He put his hand at the small of her back, because he couldn't not touch her, and they made their way to the glass doors at the other end of the room. They opened out to a sheltered patio that overlooked the water. It was chilly, but he figured he'd keep her warm.

As soon as they were outside she took an audible breath. Sympathy filled him. "Is that the first time you've breathed all evening?"

She gave him a rueful smile. "Seems like it. Old habits. I never wanted to do anything that might draw attention to myself. I always wanted to be anywhere but here."

"I can understand that." Seeing her interact with her family—except for her brother—was eye-opening.

"Can you?" She leaned on the railing and the position allowed him a fantastic view of her breasts. He shifted position slightly so he could see better—if he chose to look—and so no one coming up next to them would get the same treat.

"You don't think I can?"

"I don't know. My childhood was so lonely. I didn't have a Rose. As you can see, I didn't even have normal parents." She didn't look at him. "What was yours like?"

He rested a hip on the railing. "Normal, I guess. Both parents—though they got divorced when I was twelve. My brother and sister. All of them live downstate, around Detroit. After the divorce things changed, but our parents took a lot of trouble to make sure we knew we were loved." Really, they'd been lucky. He could see that now, in Lainey's wistful expression.

She was quiet for a moment. "I'm sorry about my dad. I'm not sure what got into him."

"He wants what's best for you." The words caused an ache in his chest. It wasn't him. But part of him—a huge part—wished it was.

Her laugh was low and sad. "If that's true, they should know Daniel's not what's best. The man's a snake." She turned and looked up into his eyes. "There's no chance of reconciliation, by the way."

While he truly hadn't thought so, relief still trickled through him. "You definitely deserve better than a snake."

A smile tugged at the corners of her mouth. "Aw. That's so sweet."

He touched her chin. *You are the sweet one,* he wanted to say. Actually, he wanted to say much more than that, and it worried him. The band struck up a slower tune and he held out a hand. "Dance with me?"

She looked up, startled. "Out here?"

"We can go inside if you'd rather. But there are more eyes."

"Good point." She turned to face him and he pulled her into his arms, then steered her away from the railing into the deeper shadows caused by the overhang of the roof.

She felt so good in his arms. She fit so well. He tried not to think of the other night, when they'd moved together in perfect sync. He pulled her closer and felt her stiffen slightly. It shouldn't matter, but it did.

He lowered his head to her ear. "You can relax. I don't bite."

She gave a half-giggle, half-sigh, and he was pleased to feel her body relax a little. "I know. I'm sorry. Just trying to get through this..." Her voice trailed off as he tugged her a little closer, so her breasts touched his chest. Her breath hitched just a bit and she shivered.

"Cold?" His voice was low, and he pulled her in even closer. She'd be able to feel, now, just how affected he was by her. What he couldn't tell her was how right she felt in his arms, how much he felt as if he'd finally come home.

"Not at all," she breathed, and tipped her face up to his.

Unable to help himself, he pressed a kiss on her soft mouth. Two things crossed his mind.

He was in trouble.

And, after all she'd done for him, she deserved to know the truth.

CHAPTER ELEVEN

THE MOMENTS SPENT in Ben's arms were magical. Almost as magical as the other night. Lainey hadn't thought dancing could be so intimate, but somehow they were in their own little world of two. She didn't want it to end, and that was a first. But, since the band had taken a break for her mother to announce the winners of the silent auction, maybe it was time to take their own personal party elsewhere.

"Do you want to leave?"

Ben's arm was draped across the back of her chair and he brushed his fingers over her bare shoulder. "This is your shindig, Laine. You know the protocol better than I do."

She leaned forward to pick up her clutch from the table. "Then let's go. My feet are killing me."

His low chuckle warmed her. "Sacrifice over?"

"Something like that." She scanned the crowd.

"I'll have to say goodnight to my mother. Give me a minute to track her down."

"I'll go with you." He unfolded himself from his chair and offered her his arm. She took it. All the vibes he gave off were those of a man who liked her, desired her—yet there was a layer underneath she couldn't quite get to…a place he kept away from her. It contrasted sharply with the intimacy of the evening. With how badly she wanted to open her heart to him.

How afraid she was, after tonight, that she already had.

Lainey found her mother near the auction exhibits. "We're heading out. It was a lovely party, Mother."

"You're leaving?" Jacqui's gaze darted from Lainey to Ben and back again. "So soon?"

Lainey kept her gaze steady on her mother's. "Yes. I'm tired and my feet hurt."

"Of course. I guess in your—" she lowered her voice "—condition that's to be expected." Someone called out to Jacqui then, and she offered her cheek to Lainey, who dropped the expected kiss. "Go straight home," she instructed, and hurried off.

Lainey sighed at the words and turned to Ben. "Shall we?"

"Absolutely." He put his hand on her back again—a gesture that Lainey was starting to love for its quiet possessiveness. It didn't take long for them to get the car and head toward home.

"Will you—will you come in?" she asked when he pulled in her driveway. The bold words startled her, especially in light of how their night together had ended before. Was she really willing to have him run away again?

He turned to her, and by the light of the dash she could see the pain in his eyes. "I'm not sure that's a good idea."

She sucked in a breath, the shininess of the evening tarnished. "Of course. Well. Thank you for everything." For the dances. For the kisses. For the feeling that this was actually going to be able to go somewhere when he must not feel the same. How could she have read it all so wrong?

He reached over the console and caught her hand as she fumbled for the door handle. "No. Lainey. Wait. I just don't want to hurt you."

She stared at him. They were in this far too deep for that. "We're adults. I know you're leaving, Ben. I know this isn't forever." But given the chance she'd take forever. The thought rocked her.

He rubbed his thumb over her lower lip and she closed her eyes.

"I can't stay the night."

The hesitation in his voice made her open them again. "All I was going to offer was coffee."

He laughed and rested his forehead on hers. "Lainey... God. I don't deserve you."

He got out of the car, and as he walked around to her door she whispered, "Yes, you do."

"Did you tell her yet?"

Ben put the leftover roast back in the fridge. For two people, they had enough to feed them for a week. Maybe two. "Tell who what?"

Rose wheeled around and he saw her frown. "Don't play games with me, Benjamin. When are you going to tell Lainey about Jason?"

He shut the fridge and stared at the sandwich he no longer had an appetite for. He was tired, he wanted to get out of the tux, and he had no idea why his grandmother had waited up for him.

"I'm not, Grandma. She doesn't need to know." He didn't want her to think less of him.

Her gaze went to slits. "Oh, yes, she does. You are in love with that girl—"

Panic sliced through him. "She's hardly a girl—" *That* was what he protested? He'd meant to say no way was he in love with Lainey. Sure, she'd helped him open up in ways he hadn't thought were possible, but that didn't mean he was in love with her.

His grandma waved his words away impatiently. "Semantics. When you're my age a thirty-something woman is a girl. You love her—even if you aren't willing to admit it yet. She's got it equally bad for you. I would have thought going with her tonight would help you see that. You don't have forever, Ben. Ask Callie."

Her voice was quiet, and Ben sank down in a chair as if she'd taken an axe to his knees. "Geez, Grandma, how can you say that?"

She wheeled closer, her gaze intense. "Do you think Jason wasted one single minute when he first spotted that girl? No, he didn't. He had some good years with her, loved her fully. And he—he alone—was reckless and lost it all. How do you think Callie would feel, knowing you are throwing your own chance at love away because her husband is gone? Is that going to make her feel better? Bring Jason back?"

Her words pinged around in him, echoing in his head. "I— No, of course not."

She poked him in the chest. "Listen to me. I know a thing or two about love, having been married to your grandpa Harry for fifty-odd years. You've found a woman who'd give you everything. You're walking away because Jason isn't here. Ask yourself—would he divorce Callie if the roles were reversed?"

He shook his head and stood up. "Of course he wouldn't. But it's not that easy, Grandma. He went in that building after me. I shouldn't have been there to begin with. It was my job to keep him safe." *I failed him.*

"It was a miscommunication that was out of your control and not your personal responsibility," she said simply. "He made a choice. He knew the risks. You both did. It's part of the job. You weren't his babysitter. You need to go see Callie. But first you need to accept that it's time to move on."

He went cold. See Callie? See first hand the destruction he'd caused? He hadn't even been able to face returning her calls. He wasn't sure he'd be welcome, that she'd want to see him. He didn't want to make things worse for her, for her kids. For Jason's sake. For her own.

For his.

But this wasn't about him.

Rose laid a hand on his arm. "You need to accept that it's okay to move on," she said quietly. "You're a good man. You deserve Lainey, and Lord knows both of you deserve to be happy. Even beyond that, she needs you and you need her. Don't let it slip away."

Her words rang true. But he didn't know if he was capable of being the man Lainey and her baby deserved. The risk of failing them was far too great. He'd failed Jason, and by extension Callie.

When he closed his eyes all he saw was Lainey. All he heard was her laugh, her voice. He could still feel her in his arms. But he couldn't be in love with her. He'd shut that part of himself down for good.

Hadn't he?

* * *

It was time to sign the paperwork.

Lainey'd read over the pages from Jon and asked Beth's husband, who was a lawyer, to look over them as well. While technically she'd need to take him to court to finalize the custody transfer, it should be able to be handled with lawyers only. This was the necessary first step to being well and truly free of her baby's father. She signed them and put them away, both relieved and a little sad.

She went into the kitchen and had just started a pot of coffee—decaf, of course—when there was a knock on the front door. She padded over that way and took a look through the peephole.

Daniel stood on the front step.

Lainey inhaled sharply and leaned her head on the door. She'd love to ignore him, but her car was in the driveway instead of the garage. And she knew he wouldn't go away.

She opened the door. "This is a bad time, Daniel. I'm really tired."

He looked her over, his gaze both hot and contemptuous, and she gripped the door tighter.

"I just want to talk."

He tried the old charming smile, but it did nothing but annoy her. She crossed her arms. "Try again. We've got nothing left to say to each other. Why are you really here, Daniel?"

He dropped all pretense. "You're pregnant." He nearly spat the words.

Her pulse picked up in warning. "Yes, I am."

"How are you going to raise it by yourself?" He stepped a little closer and she forced herself to hold her ground. "You'll be a single mother. Who's going to raise it with you?"

Ben. Oh, if only. "I'm going to be a single mother, yes. Did you need something? Because I've got things to do—"

He interrupted her. "You're making a mistake, Lainey. Your parents have opened their house to you. They're trying to help you. We all are. Don't you see? I can take care of the money problems you have. You won't have to do anything you don't want to do."

Anger spiked. "I won't have to do what? Work at a job I love? Something that has meaning to me? That I get up each morning and *want* to do? Why do you want to take that from me?"

He blinked at her. "No one's taking anything

from you. We're offering solutions so you don't have to struggle anymore. Especially now that you are pregnant."

"What I need is to make my own solutions," she said simply. "Not have yours forced on me. And the fact you can't see that means you don't know me at all. You never did."

He frowned and put his hands in his pockets. "Of course I knew you. You were my wife for seven years."

And in all that time you never picked out one birthday gift. She shook her head. "I was a tool. I was the means to an end—which was my father." Funny how she couldn't muster up any fire. She truly didn't care. He was so far behind her now he'd never catch up.

His expression radiated sincerity, but she knew better than to believe it. "I'm sorry you felt that way, Lainey. I cleaned some things up before I came here. I've changed. I made a mistake or two. You of all people know what it's like to make mistakes."

The words hit home. Still. "Yes. I do. But my baby isn't one of them. Also, I never hurt anyone or deceived anyone like you did. You made a mockery of our marriage. Of me. And that's why, even if I'd ever loved you, I wouldn't get back with you. *That* would be the biggest mistake of my life." She stepped back. "Now, if you'll excuse me, my coffee is ready."

Daniel crowded closer and stepped inside the door. His tone was wheedling. "No, wait. It was good with us, Lainey. It's better for a baby to have a father. We can have some of our own."

"No." She'd never inflict a man like Daniel on a poor kid. No child deserved that. "You need to leave. Now."

Daniel grabbed her by the upper arms, and when she tried to pull away he dug in harder. She swallowed a yelp of pain. "Lainey. This is what works best for me. For both of us. You—"

The door banged open and Daniel let go of her in surprise. Ben stood there, and the smoldering anger on his face took Lainey's breath away.

"Get away from her." The words were a low growl.

Daniel reached for her again. "Lainey, listen—"

"Get out," she hissed. "Don't come back."

Ben took a menacing step toward Daniel and

he took a step in the right direction. "She asked you to leave."

Daniel scowled, cursed, and slammed out the door.

She turned to Ben, willing her heart to return to normal, unsure if it was pumping so hard from the encounter with her idiot ex or Ben's very intoxicating nearness. "Why are you here?"

"I was in the neighborhood and saw him through the door." He shoved his hands in his pockets. "I thought you could use backup."

She pressed her hands to her face. "I wish everyone would stop trying to help me. I had it under control."

"Of course," he murmured. "I saw him handling you and jumped to conclusions."

She laid her hand on his arm as he turned to go. "No. Please. I'm sorry. I'm just so sick of my family interfering. You did me a favor by showing up here. It's not the first time he's handled me roughly."

His eyes went to slits. "He abused you?"

"No." She shook her head. "He'd grab me, like you saw tonight, but he almost never touched me.

In any manner." Then she blushed as it hit her what she'd admitted.

Ben touched her face and the delicious roughness of his fingers on her skin caused a little shiver to run down her back. "Lainey. How could he be married to you and not see what he had?"

Her gaze pinged to his at his words and the rawness in his voice and she barely dared to breathe. The reverence she saw there made her want to cry. Daniel had never looked at her like that. Ever.

She clasped his wrist and turned into his touch. "I don't think he ever saw me, Ben. That's not what he wanted."

Ben didn't get that. He looked at her and wanted everything. Wanted the whole package. Wanted the baby, the chance to be a father. It was killing him. He didn't know how to reconcile things so he could have it. *Jason, dead. Lainey, pregnant. Baby, not his.* They all bothered him and worried him and he didn't know how to move forward. She looked at him with those big eyes and he wanted to take her in his arms, into his bed, and let her soothe away the pain. Only letting go of it all seemed like a betrayal to Jason. And dumping it on her was more than he could ask of her.

Would she think less of him? He couldn't deny it mattered, even though he wished it didn't.

"Ben?"

He looked into her worried face and couldn't help the question. He needed to know. "So he's not the father?"

Her head snapped up and she laughed—a sharp bark. "God, no." She stepped away and shut the door. "Can I get you something? A drink?"

He smelled coffee. "Coffee's fine."

He followed her to the kitchen, trying and failing to keep his gaze off her perfect ass in those clingy black pants. He leaned in the doorway while she opened cupboards and lifted slightly on her toes to get mugs. The movement pulled her shirt snug across her breasts and the slight swell of her belly. He wanted nothing more than to pull her against him, hold her tiny bump in his hands. The longing nearly brought him to his knees.

She poured the coffee with a slightly shaking hand, and he accepted his. She got out milk, sugar and spoons, and led him to the small table in the dining room. He sat opposite her and watched as she doctored her coffee.

"Let me tell you about my baby's father. This is not a story I'm proud of," she said quietly, and took a deep breath. Then she poured out the whole thing, without meeting his gaze.

Ben cursed. "He didn't tell you he was married?"

She stirred her coffee without taking her eyes off the mug. "Nope. And I didn't figure it out. Pathetic, I know."

"He is. You're not." When her head came up and she opened her mouth he held up a hand. "Let me see if I've got this right. You were recovering from a marriage that was completely loveless and lacking in affection or respect of any kind. This guy showed up and took advantage of that. How is that *you* being pathetic?"

She stared into her mug. "I just should have known better."

"Oh, honey." The endearment startled him, but he meant it. "No. He took advantage of you. That's not on you."

"I could have said no." She shut her eyes. "It

wasn't like I really wanted him. It was just the idea of someone actually wanting me."

"Yeah." He pulled her to her feet. "But if you had said no, you wouldn't have this." He laid his hand on her belly and her eyes went wide. She laid her hand on top of his. "Would you wish this away?"

"Never," she said quietly. She took a deep breath. "The only thing I'd wish for is a better father for him or her. Someone like you." The words were nearly a whisper, and her soft gaze caught his.

He froze as if ice had formed in his muscles. "No, Lainey, not like me. I'm no good for you, for a baby." He wasn't what she needed. Not anymore.

She saw the shields come down and all but heard the resounding clang as they locked into place. She forced herself to hold his gaze and pressed his trembling hand against her belly. He wanted this, wanted her. She knew it—could see it. Had been seeing it as they'd gone through the past couple weeks. She wanted him too, even knowing how impossible the situation was.

"Why not?"

He slid his hand out from under hers and stepped away. The coldness she felt was as much at the loss of contact as it was for his emotional shutdown. "I can't talk about it."

She gave a little laugh and fought against the burn of tears. "Oh? But it's okay for me to spill my shames to you? It's a one-way street?"

"It's not that simple." His voice was low.

She lifted her chin. "My problems aren't simple."

"No. No, they're not," he agreed. "I meant it's not—it's not something I can talk about."

That destroyed look was back, and her heart ached. She was falling in love with this man, and he would never let her close enough to help. To love him as he deserved. As he needed.

She thought of the nightmare but didn't bring it up. The fact he chose to shut her out hurt, but what claim did she have to him? They'd been physical, she was emotionally invested, but there was no actual commitment—nothing that would mean he should tell her what had happened.

Still. She had to try. "You don't have to carry this alone," she said quietly. "Whatever it is."

He stared at a spot on the wall, but she doubted

he was seeing anything in the room. "Some things have to be," he said finally, and the pain in his voice burned in her heart. He shoved a hand through his hair. "I'm sorry, Lainey. It's just so damn hard to talk about."

She got out of her chair and moved to kneel next to him. He wouldn't look at her. "Why?" she asked, and held her breath.

His jaw worked. "I killed my best friend, okay?" At her sharp whimper he looked her in the eye. "I made a stupid mistake and a great guy died. A family man. He left his wife and two little kids. Sons who will never know their daddy now because of a mistake *I* made."

Pain washed through her—for him, for the man's family. She wanted to climb in his lap and hold him, but settled for touching his face, feeling the roughness of stubble under her hand. "Oh, Ben. I'm so sorry."

His eyes glittered with unshed tears as he looked at her. "Not as sorry as I am. I'm not the man you want, Lainey."

"Don't you think I get to decide that?" she asked, and tugged him to his feet. He let her, and she slid her arms around him, rested her head on his chest and squeezed her eyes shut as she listened to the pounding of his heart beneath her cheek. The warmth of him seeped into her pores and pooled in her heart. He stood very still for a moment, then wrapped his arms around her, too. She hoped he would allow himself to take comfort from it, from her.

They stood that way for a few minutes, then Lainey heard her phone ring. Ben stepped back, the moment broken. "I'd better get going. You okay?"

She looked at him and saw the careful remoteness back in his gaze. Her heart ached as she nodded and followed him through the living room to the door. "Fine."

He turned around and lifted her chin, his fingers lingering. The look in his eyes was a strange mixture of regret and affection. He leaned down and planted a hard kiss on her mouth. "You're not any kind of damaged goods, Lainey. Don't let anyone make you feel otherwise. Ever. You're an incredible woman." Then he left.

Lainey pressed her fingertips to her tingling mouth, her heart heavy as the front door clicked shut behind him. The tears she'd been fighting finally broke loose, and as she sank back down at the table, head on her arms, she had another thought.

His parting words had sounded an awful lot like goodbye.

CHAPTER TWELVE

At the end of the next day Lainey went into the little office area in the back of the store and checked her books. The familiar feeling of dread pooled as she added up the numbers. Better, but not good enough. She could chart steady progress upward, though, so that was hopeful. But was it enough?

"What's the verdict?" Beth walked over.

Lainey leaned back so her friend could see the screen and rested her hands on her belly. "Better. Definitely better. But not there. Yet."

Beth hesitated. "Mark and I were talking. If you're interested, we can probably swing me buying in if you want a partner."

Stunned, Lainey stared at her friend. "I— Beth, I hadn't—"

Beth held up a hand. "I know you want to do this all on your own. But you can be a success even with a partner. It doesn't make it less because you have help." She smiled and touched Lainey's shoulder. "Think about it, okay?"

"I will," she promised.

After Beth left, she stared at the numbers on the screen. Beth buying in would mean a new cooler. Repairs on the van, which even today had given her fits about going into gear. Bigger payments to her parents and therefore being out from under their thumb earlier.

Excitement and hope flared.

It was tempting. But was it the right decision?

She stood and paced out into the shop. She took in the silk flowers, the cheery Halloween-themed window. Sure, the carpet was worn, and the cash register was old but completely reliable. The fresh scent of the flowers overlaid everything and made it feel almost homey. This place was more than just a business. She loved it— loved all of it. It suited her to a T. Because of that, she couldn't let it go under. What good was it to be determined to prove herself if ultimately it sank her? That would only prove her parents right and she'd be back where she started.

She'd gone too far to let it all go under now.

She took a deep breath and walked into the

backroom. Beth was right. She just needed to make sure the numbers were stable enough for her friend to take the risk. And then she and Beth and Mark would look them over together. She wouldn't let them buy in if it turned out to be too risky. She wanted to succeed, but she was pragmatic enough to realize she wasn't out of the woods just yet.

A lightness she hadn't felt in a very long time crept into her heart. This was the right thing to do. Too bad she'd been so damn blind she hadn't been able to see it. Or maybe she hadn't been *ready* to see it. She owed Beth for putting it all into perspective.

After leaving work, Lainey pulled into Rose's driveway. She'd promised to take her friend to bingo. Ben's truck sat there, and she tried to quash the silly little spurt of anticipation. She'd stop in and say hello. Sort of face the elephant in the room head-on—see if his confession to her had done any good for him.

The light in the garage indicated he was in there, even though the big door was shut. She opened up the side door and stepped inside, almost holding her breath. How this went depended on how he looked at her when he saw her.

Her heart sank when he turned. His face was the polite mask he'd worn when she'd first met him. "Lainey."

"Hello, Ben." She kept her voice steady with effort. Two could play this game. He just looked at her and waited. "I just—wanted to see how you were. After last night." Darn it, she sounded tentative. But his impassive expression wasn't helping.

"How should I be?" He kept his gaze on her. Completely shuttered. "Nothing's changed, Lainey, if that's what you're asking."

Well, that was to the point. "Okay, then," she said stiffly. "See you around."

And she left the garage, slamming the door behind her. Not the most mature of moves, but the man frustrated her no end.

On the short walk to the house she took a couple of deep breaths, hoping Rose wouldn't notice her mood. She didn't want to be quizzed—just wanted to lick her wounds in peace.

No such luck. Rose took one look at her as soon as she entered the kitchen and frowned. "Okay.

First Ben, now you. That boy's been in a serious funk all day. What happened? He won't tell me."

Lainey blanched but managed a small smile. "Nothing happened."

Rose shook her head. "Oh, no. I may be old, but I'm neither blind nor stupid. There's much more than that, isn't there?" She sat back and examined Lainey. "Did he tell you about Jason?"

She gave a little nod. "I don't know what to tell him, Rose."

Her friend gave a little sigh. "There's really not much to say. He's got a lot to work out. On top of that, nothing ties a man up in knots more than when a relationship that was supposed to be casual turns out not to be."

Lainey gave a little shrug that she hoped was casual, even though she felt anything but. "It's the wrong time."

Rose gave a decidedly unladylike snort. "It's always the wrong time. You don't get to pick when or who you'll fall in love with, child. I see how that boy looks at you. Does he know you're pregnant?"

Despite Rose's gentle tone, the words might as well have been a shout. Lainey winced. "Yes.

How did *you* know?" Had Ben told Rose after she'd asked him not to?

"Not from him," Rose assured her. "I can just tell. You've changed physically. And the fact you told him should tell you something, honey."

Startled, Lainey met her friend's gaze. "Tell me what?"

"You told him before you told me," she said gently, and raised a hand when Lainey opened her mouth to protest. "No—no, wait. I'm not saying you should have told me first. But think about it. Why did you tell Ben?"

"I had to tell him why I couldn't go to the hospital for an X-ray," Lainey pointed out, but in retrospect she could see the holes in that theory. Why *had* she blurted it out?

Rose nodded. "But there were other reasons you could have given. Or, for that matter, no reason at all. He didn't need an explanation. A simple no thanks would have sufficed. He wouldn't have pushed. But you felt safe enough to tell him. Am I right?"

That was true. She hadn't needed to tell him. But feeling safe? With Ben? He made her feel anything *but* safe.

Well, that wasn't entirely true. He'd made her feel safe and cherished the night they'd spent together. The danger from Ben wasn't that he'd take her for granted, or treat her like her ex had. It was that he made her want things she couldn't have, that he couldn't give. And she wasn't willing to open herself to any more emotional destruction.

"Lainey." Rose leaned forward. "I know you've been through an awful lot. You have very little reason to trust people. The fact you told him is significant. The fact he went to that party with you is significant. He hasn't done anything social in months."

"The timing is all wrong," Lainey said again, because it was true. "He's not in any place for a relationship, and I— Well, I really need to do this on my own." Actually, she was starting to rethink that statement. If Beth bought in to her shop what counted was making it a success. The same idea applied to her personal life. Having a partner in life would be wonderful—but only if it was the right man.

Was Ben that man?

Rose sat back. "I understand. I do. I just want to see both of you happy. And if the two of you could be happy together—well, that would do my heart good."

"I'll be fine," Lainey assured her. Fine wasn't the same as happy, of course, and she doubted very much the distinction would be wasted on Rose.

Rose studied her for a long moment, then nodded. "I'm glad to hear it," she said. "We should get going. Don't want to be late for bingo."

Grateful to be off the hook, Lainey stood up and gathered her purse and keys.

As she wheeled her friend down the ramp Ben came out of the garage. Her heart gave a little leap and she was glad she was behind Rose, so her sharp-eyed friend didn't read anything that might be on her face. He gave Lainey a nod and she managed to smile back. As he came closer she could see the stress lines bracketing his mouth. She wanted nothing more in that moment than to go to him and smooth them away, to hold him and be held.

She looked away instead.

Ben helped Rose into the car and took care of the chair while Lainey slid behind the wheel. As they backed out of the driveway Rose narrowed her gaze on Ben, who stood watching them, hands in pockets. She muttered something that sounded like, "Foolish boy."

No, Lainey wanted to tell her. He's smart enough to know his limits.

And so was she.

"So, we've got a Friday wedding this week," Lainey noted. The flowers were simple and seasonal, fitting for a second wedding for both the bride and groom. They were starting on the bouquets today. "And a big order for a baptism on Sunday."

"Isn't it great?" Beth asked as she cut open a flower box. "Word is getting out. We're doing good."

Lainey agreed. Part of her was a little sad, though, that her personal life seemed to be one-hundred-eighty degrees away from her growing professional life. But to dwell on it wouldn't do her any good.

"Speaking of weddings," Beth said casually, "how's Ben?"

Lainey sent her a warning look. "Beth—"

"What?" Her friend's innocent look didn't fool

Lainey. She shook her head and Beth sighed. "Okay. I heard at the café that you and Ben were super cozy at the hospital gala." She plopped a box on the worktable and sent Lainey a mock glare. "Of course I didn't hear that from *you*. My supposed best friend and subject of such hot gossip."

Super-cozy. Well, she supposed they *had* been all wrapped up in each other and the spell of the evening. Dancing and kissing in the shadows. His car in front of her house for hours.

"I— Well, yeah. I guess it would look that way." She winced. "Don't people have anything else to talk about? Surely there were more interesting couples than Ben and I?"

Beth gave her a pitying look. "Lainey, I think the interesting part was the chemistry the two of you have. I heard that you were so hot together people were concerned you'd combust. Or maybe get down right there," she added thoughtfully, earning a playful smack from Lainey.

"Well, it doesn't matter now," she said, thinking of last night and how he'd been completely shut down. Pain lanced through her. She'd give anything to have this work out, to make it so they could be a couple.

But that wasn't an option. It was silly even to think it was.

"How is that?" Beth asked. "The guy kissed you. At least that much. But from how red you just turned I'm guessing it's much more than that. He helped you move. He took you to a formal party on short notice. Guys don't just do that for women they aren't interested in."

"His grandma sent him to help me," Lainey muttered. Beth didn't know how far things had gone with them, but they must have been giving off some pretty serious vibes at the gala. "And that first kiss was a pity kiss."

"Pity kiss?" Beth raised her brow. "Oh, come on, Laine. Ben doesn't seem like that type. He's so reserved. He's not going to go around kissing women because he thinks it will make them feel better."

Beth had a point. Still… "I meant it was just the moment." They'd had a lot of wonderful moments that she held on to tightly. Privately.

"Moment or not—and I think you are withholding key information from me, but I'll let it go this time—there's clearly something between you. The question is, what are you going to do about it?"

A little shiver ran through Lainey. That was the question. What *was* she going to do? She knew what she wanted, but not what he wanted. She stuffed a 'mum in florist foam with a little more force than was necessary and nearly bent it. "I'm not going there, Beth."

Beth touched her arm. "All kidding aside, why not?"

She widened her eyes. "You know why, Beth. Look at my marriage. Look at how I got in this situation. I'm doing this alone. I'm barely hanging on. There's no way he and I could make it work, even if I wanted it to. I need to keep him at a distance." She wouldn't tell Beth about Jason. It wasn't her story to tell.

"So you'll shut him down?" Beth said quietly.

She winced. Actually, he'd shut *her* down. More or less.

Beth continued. "But you don't *have* to do this alone. That's the whole point. Okay, so maybe Ben's not the guy for you. I don't know one way or the other. Chemistry is wonderful, but definitely not the only thing to base a relationship on. But don't shut yourself off all the way. Single parenting is hard. You might want someone to share it with."

"I—" She'd love to share it with Ben. She didn't see another man coming into her life whom she'd want more. But it didn't look as if that was to be. Unable to finish her sentence, she cleared her throat and changed the subject. "Well, we've got a lot to do here. Let's get these done so the bride can relax."

Beth looked as if she wanted to say something, but simply shook her head instead.

Lainey knew she was a coward. But it seemed like the only way to protect herself.

That night, Lainey had just propped her feet on the coffee table and turned the TV on when a knock sounded at the door. She padded over and peeked through the peephole to see her parents standing there. It wasn't like them to drop by unannounced. She frowned as she opened the door.

"Is everything okay?"

"Of course. Do you have a minute?" Her father's voice was strangely formal. "We won't stay long."

"I—yes, I do." She stepped aside to let them in and tried to tamp down a little surge of nerves. There could be no good reason for this visit.

Jacqui looked around the room as she slipped off her shoes. Lainey looked too—she was proud of the home she had created. A fire crackled in the hearth, and the low light of the lamps cast a warm glow over the space. She took a seat on the slip-covered couch. Panda was draped across the back. The cat didn't even crack an eye open.

Her parents sat in the chairs while Lainey muted the TV. Frankly, *Survivor* was a great backdrop for her wranglings with her parents. She set the remote carefully on the end table, dismayed to note her hand shook slightly.

"Can I get you anything?" she asked, and they both shook their heads.

"This is certainly—cozy," Jacqui said carefully, and Lainey sighed. In this case, "cozy" wasn't a compliment.

"I think so," she said, choosing to ignore her mother's meaning. "I love it."

"Well." Always one to cut to the chase, her father leaned forward. "We've got some information you might find interesting."

Her heart kicked up a bit. "Information? About what?"

Her parents exchanged a look. "About Ben Lawless, dear," her mother said.

Lainey tensed. Oh, God. They'd dug into his past. She kept her voice level as she said, "Really?"

"Yes." Jacqui pulled some papers out of her monster bag and held them out. Lainey took them reluctantly. "I think you'll find it interesting reading."

Lainey laid the pages on the couch next to her. She couldn't bring herself to look too closely at them. *Local Firefighter Under Fire* was the heading on the first page. Poor Ben.

"Why are you doing this?" She tried to keep her voice steady but failed.

"So you can see once and for all why it's a bad idea to get mixed up with him. Lainey, he's directly responsible for the death of a fellow firefighter. Ben went in after being told not to. The other man went after him. As a result, a young family man is dead. Ben's been removed from the squad. He's had some mental health issues as well. He's not stable. It's in your best interests to stay away from him." She nodded at the papers. "It's all there."

Lainey sucked in a breath. "Oh, Mother. How could you? This is beneath you."

Jacqui recoiled and flushed slightly, and looked at her husband. Greg cleared his throat. "You don't want to get mixed up with an unstable man, honey. You deserve better."

Lainey stared. Surely they couldn't mean Daniel. "A lying, cheating man who threatens me is a better choice?"

Greg winced slightly. "No. Of course not. But if Ben isn't stable you could be hurt. And you've got a child to think about. You're going to be a mother. It's time you were responsible and made better choices."

Lainey's mouth fell open. She snapped it shut. "While I appreciate you looking out for me, I'm perfectly capable of making decisions for myself. You don't know Ben. I do. He's a far better man than Daniel. Than most men. He's got honor, integrity and loyalty in spades. Not to mention he actually *listens* to what I say and doesn't make any attempt to manipulate me. He's a good man, and I never thought I'd find one like him. As for this—he's told me himself."

She stomped over to the fireplace and placed the papers on the flames. They went up with a *whoosh*. If only it were that easy to help Ben be free of his demons. When she spun back around she saw her parents staring at her and realized with a sinking feeling she'd said far, far too much.

"You're in love with him." Jacqui's tone was shocked. "What do you think he can possibly give you?"

Her mother's words stymied her. *In love with Ben?* She couldn't be. Could she? She'd been trying so hard not to be, teetering on the edge but holding her heart in reserve.

She swallowed and tried to focus. "He can't give me anything right now," she said, and heard the sorrow in her voice. "But then again he never said he could." *And I've never asked.* She'd been afraid of the answer. Just as she'd been afraid to admit she was flat-out in love with the man.

Jacqui simply stared at her, her throat working. Greg stood and pulled his wife to her feet. "Lainey, for your sake I hope this infatuation passes quickly. You've got a lot going on, trying to keep your shop going and getting ready for the baby. If you have a prayer of making this work you need to let Ben go. He's not the man for you."

"You're wrong," Lainey said, her voice quiet. She met her parents' gazes squarely. "He *is* the man for me." She knew it with all her heart. What she didn't know was how to make him understand it.

Greg herded a sputtering Jacqui out the door and Lainey sank back on the couch. In love with Ben.

She squeezed her eyes shut tightly. She'd been doing her best to ignore the truth, but there it was. She was in love with him—in all likelihood had been since they'd skipped stones at the lake. When he'd been so gentle with her. When he'd kissed her the first time.

Tears burned at the back of her throat. It was no good to love someone who had no idea how to accept it. Who was held up by the past, by something he couldn't let go.

She had to hope he loved her too, and would be willing to work through his past to give them a future. But what if he wasn't?

CHAPTER THIRTEEN

"LAINEY." HER MOTHER stood in the doorway of The Lily Pad, clearly agitated. "We need to talk. Can you take a break right now?"

Startled, Lainey took a few steps toward her mother. She hadn't thought she'd see her parents for a while after last night's little ambush had been thwarted. She'd never seen the older woman so distraught. "Mom? Are you all right?"

Jacqui shook her head. "I just—we really need to sit down and discuss this."

Beth hurried over to Lainey. "I can cover this right now. Why don't the two of you go ahead?"

Her eyes searched Lainey's face, and Lainey saw the concern there. If she disagreed, and opted to stay instead of talking to her mother, Beth would back her up. In light of last night's conversation with her parents, her mother's arrival this morning was a bit of a surprise.

She squeezed her friend's hand. To her mother

she said, "Okay. How about Mel's?" It wasn't fully private, but this time of day—mid-morning—business at the café should be a little slower.

Jacqui nodded. "That's fine."

Surprised, Lainey grabbed her coat and followed her mother out the door. She didn't think she'd ever seen Jacqui go to Mel's.

They walked in silence though the October chill. Halloween was only a couple days away, and November apparently had chosen to make an early appearance this year. Inside the warm café, Lainey led Jacqui to a corner table in the hopes they'd be undisturbed. They ordered hot drinks and sat in silence until the steaming mugs were delivered. Jacqui tapped her nails on the table relentlessly, a show of nerves Lainey didn't think she'd ever seen before.

Not wanting to wait any longer, Lainey reached over and touched her mother's hand. Jacqui looked more haggard, more tired, than Lainey could ever remember seeing her. "Mom, what's this about?"

Jacqui fussed with her coffee, then lifted her gaze to meet Lainey's. "I need you to explain how things got this way. How you could be so careless..." Her words trailed off.

"Careless as in getting pregnant? Or about Ben?" She hadn't been careless either way.

Jacqui nodded. "Either. Both. And you won't tell anyone who the father is!"

Lainey sat back. She had to choose her words carefully. "Mom, I wouldn't say I was careless. No, it wasn't planned. But it's not a mistake. As for the father..." She hesitated. She clearly had to say something, but what? She settled for an abridged version of the truth. "Well, he's not interested in being in our lives. He's got his reasons, and none of them are anything I want my child associated with." She hesitated just for a second before adding, "Why do you keep pushing Daniel on me?"

Jacqui looked her straight in the eye. "Because he can take care of you. And now the baby, too. It's going to be so hard for you to raise the child and run that shop. I'm sure he'd let you keep the store, and you can work when you want. But you wouldn't have to worry about money. Are you *sure* the baby's father is out of the picture?"

Lainey thought of the papers she'd signed with

a little pang of sorrow mixed with relief. "Yes." She crossed her arms on the table and leaned forward. "Mom. I understand you want me to be taken care of. I do. And I appreciate your concern. But Daniel's not the way to do it. I'm managing—working things out. It won't be easy, but I'm going to make it work. You and Dad need to just let me do it."

Jacqui was silent for a long moment, fiddling with her untouched coffee mug. Then she said, "I just don't understand why you'd want to struggle when you don't have to. When there are people who can give you so much."

Lainey saw the puzzlement on her mother's face and knew she truly *didn't* understand. "It's not that I want to struggle. It's that I want to do something on my own. When you guys step in and try to take over you attach strings and conditions and you take the power away from me. It's not mine, then. Being a single mother isn't ideal. It will make everything a lot harder, to be sure. But that's how it's going to be, Mom. I can't change that." She took a deep breath and thought of Ben with a sharp pang. "If I ever get married it will be because I love the man, and because he loves and respects me for who I am—not who I come from or what I can do for him. Does that make sense?"

Jacqui clasped her hands tightly in front of her for a moment. Finally she lifted her chin. "Yes," she said quietly. "It does. Does Ben know how you feel?"

Lainey dropped her gaze to her mug of tea. Her heart squeezed. "I don't think so."

Her mother pushed her mug out of the way and leaned toward her. "Then you need to tell him. Sooner rather than later. Why would you let him walk away?"

Lainey's jaw actually dropped. "Mother…" she managed. "I— Whoa. I thought you were against Ben?"

Jacqui reached over and covered Lainey's hand with her own. "We don't want you to have to struggle when you have the opportunity to avoid it. But you need to be happy, too. It's been so long—" She stopped for a moment, then sighed. "I love your father, even with all his faults. When you talk about Ben you light up. The way you defended him last night—well, you should have the chance to see where that leads you. I'm sorry for making it so difficult for you."

It was quite possibly the first time her mother had ever really listened and actually heard what Lainey was saying. She got up and pulled her mother into an awkward hug, right there in Mel's. Her mother's quiet words were as good as Jacqui could do, and Lainey was willing to accept them as a start.

Her mother patted her awkwardly on the back. "Go get him," she said, and Lainey's eyes got damp. "And, please, if we can help let us know. I'll try not to shove myself where I've got no business being."

Lainey stepped back and laughed even as she swiped at her eyes. "Thank you." Jacqui wouldn't understand, but that was the nicest thing her mother had ever said to her.

"All right, then." Her mother gathered her bag and her coat. "I mean it. If we can help with the shop and the baby let us know."

"I will," Lainey murmured. She didn't want their help, if at all possible, but having it offered rather than rammed down her throat was a huge improvement. She tried and failed to picture her parents babysitting. The thought almost made her giggle. Maybe they'd come around.

She hurried back to work. Beth was ringing up a sale, but by the time Lainey got her coat off and went back out front was already heading for her. "How did it go?"

Lainey reached for the watering can. "It was fine, actually. She made an effort to listen to me. I'm not sure she understands why I feel the way I do, but she seems willing to accept it. It's some small steps in the right direction." She'd take the olive branch and hope it held. To have her parents work with her rather than at cross-purposes would make everything so much easier.

That evening was pizza night with Rose. Lainey was half tempted to cancel. She was so tired, and the thought of seeing Ben and simply exchanging polite words, pretending there'd never been more between them, was just too hard.

But she picked up the usual pizza and headed out. She'd do her best to put on a happy face.

Ben was nowhere to be found when she pulled in, and relief tempered with a good dose of disappointment flooded through her. She tried to push it all away. She was here for Rose only, and had been long before he'd come back. She would be long after he'd left again.

"Come on in!" Rose called when Lainey knocked.

She pushed the door open and fixed a smile on her face which faltered when she spotted Ben's jacket draped over a chair. How far gone was she when the sight of a fleece could almost reduce her to tears? She busied herself putting the box on the counter and removing her own coat while making small talk. She thought she'd actually done pretty well until she sat across from Rose and looked at her sympathetic face.

"Oh, dear. You've got it that bad, huh?" Rose's question was gentle.

Lainey couldn't meet her friend's eyes so she looked down at the slice of pizza she had zero interest in eating. Her answer stuck in her throat as if the words were glued there, and she was afraid if she tried to speak all her carefully rigged control would go right out the window.

The back door opened then, and Ben came in. Her gaze flew to his and Lainey would swear time stopped. Her breath caught at the pain and the longing she saw, which he quickly dropped behind the mask she was all-too familiar with. She looked away. She should have stayed home tonight. Rose would have understood.

"Pizza, Ben?" Rose's voice was overly bright, and it seemed to bounce off the tension that filled the room.

"No, thanks."

The deep rumble of his voice resonated deep in Lainey's soul. Oh, did she have it bad. Rose didn't know the half of it.

"I need this."

The jacket whooshed off the chair next to her and Lainey squeezed her eyes shut tight when she caught a bit of his scent mixed with the fresh air notes that came from spending a lot of time outside. She didn't dare look up until the door shut behind him.

Rose made a little noise of frustration in her throat. "Oh, my goodness, I'm not sure I've ever seen a couple so right for each other work so hard to avoid it! Talk to him, Lainey. Please. Don't let this get away. From either of you. You don't want to regret it later."

It wasn't quite that simple. "Rose—"

Her friend leveled her with a gentle look. "Do you love him?"

Lainey sucked in a breath. "Yes. Yes, I do." The answer was oh-so-easy, but not simple.

"He went back into the garage. Go to him. Please." Rose looked at her with shrewd eyes. "Don't waste anymore time. That little baby needs a daddy and Ben would be a wonderful one. Plus, not only does he need you—you need him."

He needs you. Lainey didn't know if that was true or not. If he needed her, how could he shut her out and hold her at arm's length? Still, she found her feet carrying her out the door to the garage. Her heartbeat picked up the closer she got to the building. Was she crazy to lay it all on the line? She hadn't come here intending to do so. Even though Rose was right. It *was* time. She couldn't go on in this half-life. She had to know.

Ben looked up when she came in, and she caught the longing in his eyes before he shuttered it. "Hi."

"Hey. How are you feeling?"

His voice was perfectly polite. She could almost see the force fields around him, trying to keep her at a safe distance. It hurt that after all they'd shared he could just lock her out.

"Okay." It wasn't a lie. Pregnancy-wise, she was. Otherwise, not so much.

He nodded, then met her gaze. "What do you need, Lainey?"

You. She took a deep breath and jumped in. "Can you tell me the rest of the story, Ben? About Jason?" Since everything seemed to hinge on his friend's death, she needed to know.

He set down the tool he'd been holding. His hands were shaking slightly. "I told you the gist of it."

"Yes, you did. But I don't know what actually happened." She moved a little closer. Her hands shook so badly she shoved them in the pockets of her coat. "I don't know exactly why you blame yourself, because from what I've seen you aren't so careless as to knowingly or intentionally lead another person into danger."

He winced, raked a hand through his hair. "Lainey—"

She kept her gaze on him steady. Kept her voice calm and didn't move any closer, so she wouldn't spook him. "Ben, please. Let me in. We've got the potential here for something wonderful, and I'd love the chance at a future with you. But with this between us we can't." She couldn't bring herself to ask if he wanted it, too. The very real chance of him saying no would destroy her.

"Don't make me a better man than I am." His words were harsh and he moved toward her, his gaze hard on hers.

She stood her ground as he stalked closer.

"I didn't get the order. Somehow there was a breakdown in the chain and I didn't get the order that the building was clear. As far as I knew there was one occupant left." He stopped, took a shuddering breath. "I went in. Jason came in after me because he recognized the signs that the situation was deteriorating rapidly. He'd gotten the order. He knew he wasn't supposed to go in." He shut his eyes. "He came in anyway. For me. When he had so much to lose. He had everything to lose. His wife—Callie. Those kids."

Lainey's eyes burned at the bleakness in his voice and she didn't even try to stop the tears. Now she got it. He blamed himself for living when his friend was dead. She came a little closer and rested her hand on his arm, feeling the tightness of the muscles beneath. He blinked at her, as if he'd forgotten she was there for a few moments, lost in his own private hell. "How can you blame yourself for Jason's choice? What does his wife say?"

He froze and then looked away, his jaw working.

Her heart sank. "Oh, no. Ben. How can she blame you?"

Misery was etched on his face. "I don't know if she does. I haven't seen her or talked to her since—since the funeral. She's called, but I haven't called her back."

Lainey inhaled sharply. "Ben, why not?"

He moved away from her, his movements agitated and jerky. "I can't, okay? What if it's the wrong thing to do?" He paused and drew in a ragged breath. "You didn't see her at the funeral. She was so—lost. She's been through so much already. I can't make it worse for her. I can't take that chance."

She shook her head. "Okay, but who are you to decide what makes it worse for her? Ben, how can you possibly know? You're a living link to Jason for her, for her kids. That's so important.

How can you leave them like that? Is that what he'd want?"

He turned around, propped his hands on his hips. "Lainey—"

She was too far in to back out now. "Go. Talk to her. See what she has to say so you can get some closure. If you can't do that we don't have a future. *You* don't have a future as a firefighter, much less as a husband. You can't punish yourself forever. You need to forgive yourself, and Jason as well. He didn't give up his life so you could spend yours all alone."

He opened his mouth, but snapped it shut when she steamrollered right over him.

"I love you. But if you can't choose me—choose a life with me over your past—then we've got nowhere to go."

She barely breathed as he stood in the middle of the garage and stared at her.

Finally he said in a low tone, "I can't risk it, Lainey."

Her heart shattered, the razor sharp edges of pain nearly bringing her to her knees. "Then you're not the man I thought you were."

It took everything she had to turn and walk away from the man she loved.

Ben stood frozen in the garage after Lainey had left. She had simply sailed out, her chin high, tear-tracks fresh on her beautiful face. He heard her car start, then the crunch of tires on the driveway.

The loss of her ripped through him. God, how could he be so damn stupid? He wanted nothing more than to go after her, tell her how much he loved her. But he couldn't.

Because he was an idiot. What kind of man let the woman he loved walk away?

One whose past held him firmly in its snare. He knew that. He'd allowed it because it meant he was able to hide, somehow thinking that would make up for the loss of his friend. Worse, he'd used it as an excuse to cement the belief he was better off alone. That was inexcusable. Even though over the past few weeks he'd been busy falling for Lainey. She'd burst right through his defenses, made him feel, made him want, and while he'd convinced himself those were the last things he wanted she'd gotten in his heart anyway.

But if you can't choose me—choose a life with me over your past—then we've got nowhere to go.

Her words echoed in his head. What kind of man chose to live in the past when the future hovered so brightly in front of him? Lainey wasn't wrong. It was past time he paid Callie a visit. Set some things right and got closure. Maybe Jason's widow needed it, too. And choosing to live his life and love Lainey seemed like a far better tribute to his friend's memory than staying in the shadows for the rest of his days.

Then he'd see if he could have a true future with Lainey. She deserved all of him—not some damaged shell. He'd prove he could move on. He pulled his phone out of his pocket, took a deep breath, and dialed a familiar number.

Beth came in and plunked down a small bakery bag. "Cheesecake muffin. Because I'm pretty sure you haven't eaten yet."

Lainey winced. "I'm trying, Beth. I'm just not very hungry."

Her friend nudged the bag closer. "I know, honey. But you've got to feed that baby."

Lainey managed a smile. "I know that. And I am." *Mostly.* Lainey opened the bag. Her appetite hadn't been stellar since her first conversation with Ben about Jason, and had virtually disappeared after their confrontation in the garage two days ago. He'd made his choice. It wasn't her.

So it was over before it really had a chance to begin.

The pain broke over her again. Every time the wave wore her down a little more. She took a shaky breath and took the bag from Beth.

"I know this is so hard for you. Can I do anything, Laine? I know I keep asking, but—" Beth broke off. "It's so awful to see you like this. Can you call him? See if you can work it out?"

Lainey managed a little smile. She knew she didn't need to pretend around Beth, but she was hoping to fool herself into thinking it wasn't as painful as she thought. "It didn't end in a way I can actually fix. He's got—he's got issues that only he can resolve. And he has to be ready to do that. I can't make him ready." And there was also the simple but excruciating fact she didn't actually know if he loved her.

Beth leaned forward. "I've seen him look at you, Laine. That man is in love with you."

"Maybe. But he never said the words, Beth." Her eyes burned with tears she did not want to shed in public. "I *think* he'd love me, if he could. But I don't really *know*. He knows how I feel." She took a shaky breath and tried to smile, even though it failed to actually form. "So I'm going to try to move on."

If only it was that easy.

"Oh, honey. I'm so sorry." Beth glanced back as the back doorbell buzzed. "Eat that. I'll get the delivery."

She left and Lainey opened the bag and removed the muffin, centering it on a napkin. She'd been through the whole thing over and over. No use going over it all for the umpteenth time. The story of a broken heart was as old as time. She'd manage to survive.

But it was a huge hole in her heart. She missed him. Missed what they'd never really had a chance to have. Missed what might have been.

That was almost as dangerous.

She broke off a small bite of muffin. Normally it was one of her favorite treats. It would take her all morning to eat it, because today she could probably eat the bag it came in and not notice any difference in taste. But Beth was right. She needed to feed the baby.

The front door chimed and Lainey's idiotically optimistic heart kicked, then crashed. It hadn't been Ben yet, and this time was no different. A smiling man approached the counter, wanting a dozen roses for his wife. Lainey put them together with a smile, but her heart ached.

"Thank you," he said as she handed him the roses wrapped in green and pink paper. "She's worth every rose you've got in your store. But I can only afford a dozen today."

Lainey gave a little laugh, but a little spear of sorrow pierced her heart. If things had been different would Ben have said the same about her? "She's a lucky woman."

He winked as he slid his wallet in his pocket. "Nah. I'm the lucky one."

Whistling, he walked out, and Lainey watched him go with a heavy heart. People clearly could make love work. Some of them overcame crazy stuff to be together.

And some of them couldn't.

CHAPTER FOURTEEN

BEN STOOD IN front of the little white bunga-
low, with its cozy front porch and dormant rose
bushes. A house not too different from the one
Lainey lived in. Pumpkins on the front steps.
Fake spiderweb on the porch. Like almost every
other house on the block.

But this one belonged to Callie and Jason.
Well, just Callie now. He swallowed hard at the
thought.

He'd come to finally make amends—something he should have done months ago.

The front door flew open and Callie stood
there, the baby—who wasn't really a baby anymore—on her hip. She looked at him steadily
and his heart thumped in his chest as he started
up the walk towards her.

"Callie." He swallowed, the words suddenly
seeming inadequate. "I'm—"

"If you say you're sorry, Ben Lawless, you cannot take another step and come in this house." Eyes blazing, Callie stepped out on the porch.

Confusion stopped him in his tracks more than her threat. "What?"

"You heard me." She jerked her head toward the door and her coppery curls bounced on her shoulders. "Come in. We need to talk and it's cold out here."

He followed her into the house, the reminder of Jason not as physical a punch as it would have been a few weeks ago. The oldest boy, Eli, who was three, looked at him out of his father's eyes and smiled his father's smile.

"Hey, buddy." Ben bent down and accepted the hug the little boy offered. His heart squeezed. He'd do better by Jason's kids if Callie would let him. He'd love to see them grow up—maybe play with Lainey's baby if she would forgive him.

"Have a seat." Callie nodded at the table which held a basket of crayons and a stack of coloring books. "Let me get them set up for a little while." To the kids she said, "How about *Bob the Builder*?" A chorus of yeses followed her words and soon cheery music wafted from the living room. She returned to stand across from him, her posture stiff.

"They'll be good for a bit now. Can I get you a drink?"

He shook his head. "Ah, no. Thanks. Callie—"

"No." She gave a sharp shake of her head, splayed her hands on the table and leaned forward. "You listen to me first—okay, Ben? I can't believe you stayed away for so long. It wasn't your fault. Jason did *not* die because of you."

Ben closed his eyes. While rationally he knew she was right that Jason had not died because of him—and a hard-won victory *that* was—being here, with Jason's young widow, he could still smell the smoke, hear the roar of the flames crackling in the back of his mind. It gave him a bad moment.

"I know that. It took me far too long to figure it out. I want to apologize for staying away so long. I never meant to. And I am terribly sorry for the loss of your husband and my friend."

"Thank you. That's an apology I will accept," Callie whispered. She threaded her fingers together. "While I know Jason for the most part followed the rules—he didn't want to be careless—he was at heart a risk-taker. Once he realized what had happened to you there was no stopping him." She took a shaky breath and Ben met her gaze, seeing the sadness in her green eyes. "He didn't think, Ben. That's the thing. He just acted. They told me—after—they told me they couldn't stop him. Nothing could have. He loved you like a brother."

"It was mutual." It was true. And he knew Callie was right about her husband. In a potential do-or-die situation there wasn't time to stand around and waffle about what action to take. He and Jason had both done the only thing they could do in the moment. If the situation had been reversed he would have done the same thing.

So many people said they'd walk through fire for their loved ones. Jason had actually done it.

The kids' laughter caused Callie to turn her head in their direction. She pulled out a chair and sank down into it. "I've been mad as hell," she said quietly. "But not at you. Or at least not about this. For staying away—that's something else entirely. Jason loved risk. I knew when I married him—well, I knew. I never thought it'd end like this, but it did." She tipped her head toward the living room. "And now they don't have a daddy. Jason didn't leave us on purpose. He wouldn't let you accept responsibility for his choices any more than you would have let him."

"I know that now," he said. "It took me a while to get there—longer than it should have. Callie—again, I am sorry. Sorrier than you know for your loss, for the boys' loss. Someone helped me see how blind I've been. It's been at your expense. I'm sorry." Lainey had been right when she'd said Jason hadn't given up his life so Ben could ignore his own.

Callie reached over and squeezed his hand, the sheen of tears in her green eyes. "Thank you for that. Please, don't be a stranger in our lives. You are such a valuable link to Jason, and I'd like the boys to know you. You can help them understand what their daddy was like as a firefighter."

"I will," he promised, relieved that the thought didn't fill him with the kind of pain he'd been accustomed to. The lightening of the load was an amazing thing, and while the apology he'd made had helped, it was Lainey who'd shown him the way.

He pulled Callie in for a hug. She hugged him back, then patted his chest.

"Who's the someone? She must be awfully special if you finally came to see me."

"Ah…" Uncomfortable, he looked into the living room, where the boys played with trucks and watched the movie. "She pointed out a few things to me that I'd been missing."

Callie gave a little laugh. "Well, I like her already. When can I meet her?"

He met her gaze. "Well, about that…"

Her eyes went to slits. "Oh, no. What did you do?"

Was he so transparent? He scrubbed his hand over his face, then gave her an abridged version of events and didn't cut himself any slack.

"Do you love her?"

"I do." There was no hesitation.

She gave him a small shove toward the door. "Then why are you still here? What you need to do is go back and see if she'll still have you." She gave him another little shove, her voice urgent. "Ben. You've got to go see if you can make it work. Don't waste any more time. You never know how much of it you have."

"I know. It's where I'm going next. Now I know—" He stopped, about to add, *what you and Jason had.* It seemed somehow cruel to bring it up.

But Callie nodded and smiled—a small smile, with tears in her eyes. "Yes. Now you know."

"I've got to go," he said. "I had to be sure you were okay."

"I'm hanging in there," she said softly. "It hasn't been easy, but I'm doing my best. I'll miss him every day for the rest of my life. But I knew my husband, Ben. I know how he was. I know *who* he was. And he's a hero."

"Yeah, he is." He drew her into another hug, rocked her back and forth. "Thanks, Callie."

She hugged him back tightly. "Go get her. Good luck."

"I will. And, God knows, I'll need it."

He left the house, with Callie standing on the porch, arms crossed against the cold, and drove away. He pointed the truck north, toward Holden's Crossing. Time to put the beginning of the rest of his life in motion. If Lainey would have him.

There was only one way to find out.

* * *

Lainey had shoved the last of the clothes in the dryer when she heard a knock on the kitchen door. It was seven-thirty on a rainy night. Who could possibly be stopping over this late? She trudged up the stairs and peeked out the peephole.

And gasped.

Ben stood there, rain glistening on his jacket. She blinked. Was it really him? Or was her mind playing tricks on her?

He knocked again and she jumped, her shaking hands making a fumbling hash of the lock and the knob. *Ben.* Why was he here? Could she take any more heartbreak? She was afraid the answer to that was no.

She swung the door open and simply drank him in. His intense gaze settled on her and she saw pain and longing there. Hope surged a little bit, but she tamped it down. He looked tired, and stress lines bracketed his mouth. Not for the first time she wanted to reach up and smooth them away.

"Lainey. Can I come in? I'll understand if you say no." His voice was a low rumble and she stepped to the side quickly, her heart hammering so hard she was afraid he'd hear it.

"Of course. I was just surprised." She shut the door behind him and turned to face him. As glad as she was to see him, a little anger flared. She welcomed it. She needed it to keep her distance from him until she knew why he was here. "Since you were pretty clear the other day that we weren't going to work out." She couldn't quite keep the bitterness out of her voice.

He let out a long exhale. The misery etched on his face echoed that in her heart. "I know. I'm sorry. I need to talk to you."

"I see. Well, come on in." Without waiting to see if he'd follow, she walked through the kitchen into the living room. She sat on a chair near the fireplace and wound her hands tightly together. The heat of the fire did nothing to soothe her nerves.

He didn't follow right away, but a thump from the kitchen area indicated he was probably removing his boots. A few seconds later he appeared and she had a hard time breathing. He seemed to fill the small space and absorb all the oxygen.

She gestured to the chair across from her. "Please sit."

He did, and she tried not to notice when he looked at her with a tenderness that nearly undid her. "Lainey. God, you're gorgeous."

She kept her gaze on his steady, even though she felt anything but steady inside. How could he say that? She'd barely slept and had no appetite. She was a mess, not to mention an emotional wreck. "Thank you." She didn't know what to say, what to ask. There was so much to say, really, she didn't know where to begin.

But, since he'd more or less rejected her, she'd let him talk first. He knew where she stood. She'd laid it out for him the other day in the garage. It was past time she could say the same about him.

He dropped his gaze, leaned forward and rested his forearms on his thighs. The awkwardness grew as he seemed to gather his thoughts. She watched the firelight dance on his dark hair. Finally, too tightly wound to wait, she gave in. She needed to know.

"Ben, why are you here?"

He looked up. "Should I be?"

The question threw her. "I don't know." Her

voice dropped to a whisper. "You made it clear the other day you couldn't choose me." Despite her earlier flare of anger, she couldn't muster any heat in the words, only pain.

He took a deep breath and sat back. Her traitor cat came and wound around his ankles. She frowned at Panda, but of course the cat ignored her. Ben reached down to stroke his hand down Panda's back. "I was pretty screwed up, Lainey. In a lot of ways. I've still got work to do. I don't know when I'll be able to work again." He looked up and in his gaze she saw pain and something else. Her heart picked up. "You're going to be a mom. You need a guy who's stable. I can barely take care of myself. How could I take care of a family?"

"So you pushed me away," she said, unable to keep the hurt from her voice. She focused on the traitor cat at his feet.

He leaned forward and laid a hand on her arm, forcing her startled gaze to his. "I did. I thought it was better for you. I wanted to protect you," he admitted. "But you just kind of worked your way in and I started wanting more. A lot more. After you left the other day I realized how blind

I'd been. I made an appointment with a counselor. And there was one last thing I needed to do."

"Callie?" she said softly.

He nodded. "I went and talked to Callie. Not for permission to move on, but because you were right. She was angry—but not for the reasons I thought. She was mad because she felt I'd abandoned her and the kids. She never blamed me. But even if I'd known that I'm not sure it would have made a difference."

His eyes were wet as he looked at Lainey and her heart broke for him.

"I blamed myself fully. But there were things that night that were out of my control, out of his control. I can't bring him back. But the way I've been living is no way to honor my best friend. Jason would kick my ass."

A surprised laugh bubbled out of her. "He sounds like a true friend."

Ben smiled. "He was. I wish you could have known him. He'd have liked you."

Tears stung her eyes. "I wish I could have, too. But—"

His smile turned sad. "But that's not how it is.

I hope I can convince you to meet Callie, though. I think you'll like her. And the kids."

She circled back to the fact that had surprised her. "You saw a counselor?"

Ben nodded. "Well, not yet. The appointment is next week. Monday. One of the terms of coming off leave is I need to get a mental health exam, I guess you'd call it. I need to know—and my captain needs to know—I won't flashback and freeze the next time I go out on a call."

She swallowed hard. That didn't sound as if he was going to stay here. "Ah. Will it work?"

He gave her a crooked smile. "I don't know. I hope so. I'd like to be cleared in a month or so. I want to go back to work."

"That's great, Ben." She meant it. But, really, did the man have to drive all the way back here to tell her this? That he wouldn't be back, after all? A phone call would have given her a little more dignity. "Well, I'm sure they'll be thrilled to have you back."

Something in her tone must have given her away, because he looked at her quizzically. "They won't."

She stared at him for a moment, not comprehending. "But you just said—"

"I know," he interrupted her. "But you're jumping to conclusions. I won't be working in Grand Rapids. I'll be here. Or almost here. In Traverse City. Holden's Crossing is close enough I can live here. The job—it's time-consuming and there's always risk."

Her heart beat faster. Had he really just said what she thought she'd heard? "Oh," she said. "Here?"

Instead of answering right away, he came to his knees on the floor in front of her and cautiously laid his hand on her rounded belly. "I know it hasn't been that long," he murmured, "but I missed you. Both of you."

Lainey laid her hand on his and held her breath. She didn't trust herself to speak. She was afraid to ask the question, more afraid of the answer.

He slid a cold hand around the back of her neck and pulled her down toward him. "I love you," he whispered. "I love both of you. I missed you. So much." Then he kissed her, soft at first, then with more urgency.

"I love you, too," she whispered against his mouth. "Ben—"

He sat back and ran one hand down the side of her face. Her heart lifted at the reverence and love on his face. "So, to answer your question, yes. Here. In this house, if you want. I want to be your husband and a father to this baby. I know it's short notice, and I've been an idiot, and—damn it—I don't have a ring and you might not be ready—"

She laid her fingers on his lips, joy coursing through her. "I'm ready." Oh, was she ever? She'd been wrong about not needing a partner in her life—she needed Ben. She hadn't even known what she was missing until he'd come into her life. "There's no one I want to be with more than you."

His eyes widened and a slow smile spread across his face. "Are you sure?"

Her voice was strong and she was pretty sure she might burst with happiness. "Yes. I want forever. And I want it with you."

"Oh, thank God." He stood up and held out a hand, a wicked gleam in his eyes. "Then I say we go celebrate. Plus, I think we've got some making up to do." He gave her a little eyebrow-wiggle that made her laugh.

"Sounds good to me. We'd better get started." Lainey put her hand in his and smiled up at him, ready to embrace their future.

Ten months later

Lainey tugged at the bodice of her wedding dress for what had to be the fifteenth time in as many minutes. "Are you sure this looks secure?"

Beth, her matron of honor and business partner, laughed and pulled Lainey's hands down. "It looks great, Laine. No one can tell you've got nursing pads in the sexy bra under it. You are a gorgeous bride." She leaned over and plucked Lainey's bouquet from the box on the table, pressed it into Lainey's hands. "Here. Now, turn and look in the mirror."

Lainey did. The woman staring back at her barely resembled herself. Flushed cheeks, sparkling eyes, flowing off-white beaded simple strapless gown. The flowers, done by Lainey herself, were a perfect complement for a summer wedding in shades of pink and cream.

Beth touched the small veil that covered Lainey's head and shoulders. "See? Perfectly gorgeous. Are you ready?"

"Very." Lainey smiled at her friend. "I can't wait."

"Then let's go." Beth exited the small room, and with a deep breath Lainey followed.

As Beth took her place at the head of the aisle Lainey paused, out of sight of the guests in the sanctuary. A well of emotion threatened to break over her as her father and brother approached her. They were here to walk her down the aisle in this small church. Amazingly, her mother had exercised great restraint and hadn't interfered with the planning or the size of the wedding. Not too much, anyway. They'd made strides—especially after the birth of baby Lily.

Rose had her three-month-old great-granddaughter in the front pew. Lainey sincerely hoped she wouldn't have to take a break mid-ceremony and nurse her daughter.

Her heart was absolutely full.

"Honey, you look amazing," her father said, his voice rough with emotion, and Lainey blinked furiously.

"Don't make me cry," she managed on a laugh, and he squeezed her arm.

"No promises, there, my girl. It's your wedding. We may not have a choice."

She gave a little giggle as Kevin came to take his place at Lainey's side. He chucked her lightly under the chin. "Ready, little sis?"

She smiled up at him. Oh, was she ever? "Yes. Yes, I am."

The music swelled and Lainey moved to the head of the aisle. She took the first few steps toward her future. Her gaze landed on Ben. Her steps nearly faltered as she took in how handsome he was in his tux and she couldn't take her eyes off him. He was hers.

Ben's gaze never left her, and she saw all the love, all the heat, all the joy in her own heart reflected on his face as she reached for his hands at the altar. Her heart swelled as she looked into his beautiful eyes.

"Hi," he whispered. "God, you're gorgeous."

She smiled back. "So are you."

Together they glanced at their daughter—the baby who was everything to Ben despite the fact she wasn't biologically his—then back at the minister, who now began the ceremony.

Somehow, despite everything, without even looking for it, they'd become a family.

Forever.

* * * * *

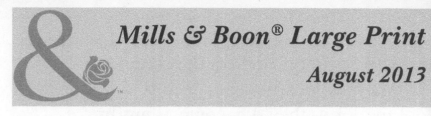

Mills & Boon® Large Print

August 2013

MASTER OF HER VIRTUE
Miranda Lee

THE COST OF HER INNOCENCE
Jacqueline Baird

A TASTE OF THE FORBIDDEN
Carole Mortimer

COUNT VALIERI'S PRISONER
Sara Craven

THE MERCILESS TRAVIS WILDE
Sandra Marton

A GAME WITH ONE WINNER
Lynn Raye Harris

HEIR TO A DESERT LEGACY
Maisey Yates

SPARKS FLY WITH THE BILLIONAIRE
Marion Lennox

A DADDY FOR HER SONS
Raye Morgan

ALONG CAME TWINS...
Rebecca Winters

AN ACCIDENTAL FAMILY
Ami Weaver

0713 Rom LP

Mills & Boon® Large Print

September 2013

A RICH MAN'S WHIM
Lynne Graham

A PRICE WORTH PAYING?
Trish Morey

A TOUCH OF NOTORIETY
Carole Mortimer

THE SECRET CASELLA BABY
Cathy Williams

MAID FOR MONTERO
Kim Lawrence

CAPTIVE IN HIS CASTLE
Chantelle Shaw

HEIR TO A DARK INHERITANCE
Maisey Yates

ANYTHING BUT VANILLA...
Liz Fielding

A FATHER FOR HER TRIPLETS
Susan Meier

SECOND CHANCE WITH THE REBEL
Cara Colter

FIRST COMES BABY...
Michelle Douglas